## PRAISE FOR QUIRK CLASSICS

### PRIDE AND PREJUDICE AND ZOMBIES
BY JANE AUSTEN AND SETH GRAHAME-SMITH

"Jane Austen isn't for everyone. Neither are zombies. But combine the two and the only question is, Why didn't anyone think of this before? The judicious addition of flesh-eating undead to this otherwise faithful reworking is just what Austen's gem needed."—*Wired*

### SENSE AND SENSIBILITY AND SEA MONSTERS
BY JANE AUSTEN AND BEN H. WINTERS

"'The effect is strangely entertaining, like a Weird Al version of an opera aria, and Eugene Smith's amusing illustrations add an extra touch of bizarre hilarity."—*Library Journal*

"It's a monsterpiece."—*Real Simple*

### ANDROID KARENINA
BY LEO TOLSTOY AND BEN H. WINTERS

"*Android Karenina* lives up to its promise to make Tolstoy 'awesomer'"—*The A.V. Club*

"Winters does a spectacular job, adding robots and mechanical terrorism to the misery, adultery, and philosophical introspection of Tolstoy's masterpiece."—*Library Journal*

"This is quite possibly the definitive mash-up novel. If anything, the sci-fi elements add to the book's feelings of isolation and humanity." —*Den of Geek*

# THE
# MEOWMORPHOSIS

BY FRANZ KAFKA
& COLERIDGE COOK

*Illustrations by*
MATTHEW RICHARDSON

**QUIRK BOOKS**
PHILADELPHIA

Library of Congress Cataloging in Publication Number: 2011921159

ISBN: 978-1-59474-503-4

Printed in Canada
Typeset in Bembo

Cover design by Doogie Horner
Cover photo courtesy the Bridgeman Art Library International Ltd.
Illustrations by Matthew Richardson
Production management by John J. McGurk

10 9 8 7 6 5 4 3 2 1

Quirk Books
215 Church Street
Philadelphia, PA 19106
quirkbooks.com
quirkclassics.com

# LIST OF ILLUSTRATIONS

# I.

One morning, as Gregor Samsa was waking up from anxious dreams, he discovered that he had been changed into an adorable kitten. He lay in bed on his soft, fuzzy back and saw, as he lifted his head a little, his brown arched abdomen divided into striped bowlike sections. His blanket, just about ready to slide off completely, could hardly stay in place as he rolled from side to side. His legs—too many!—pitifully thin compared to the rest of his rotund circumference, pawed helplessly before his eyes.

"What's happened to me?" he thought. It was no dream. His room—a proper room for a human being, only a bit too small—lay quietly between the four well-known walls. On the wall above the table, upon which was spread an unpacked collection of sample cloth goods—Samsa was a traveling salesman—hung the picture that he had cut out of an illustrated magazine a little while ago and set in a pretty gilt frame. It was a picture of a woman in a fur hat and a fur boa. She sat erect there, lifting in the direction of the viewer a solid fur muff into which her entire forearm had disappeared. Samsa felt a powerful urge to leap upon the sample cloths and scratch at them thoroughly, but as soon as it had come, it passed.

Gregor's glance then turned to the window. The dreary weather—the raindrops were falling audibly on the metal window ledge—made him quite melancholy. "Why don't I keep sleeping for a little while longer and forget all this foolishness," he thought. But this proved quite impractical, for he was used to sleeping on his back, and in his present state he couldn't get comfortable in this position. No matter how hard he threw himself onto his back, he always rolled again onto his furry side, or his belly, his haunches settling last onto his old bed. He must have tried it a hundred times, closing his eyes so he would not have to see the waggling paws, and gave up only when he began to feel a light, dull pain in his side that he had never felt before.

"O God," he thought, yawning and stretching his front paws. "What a relentless job I've chosen! Day in, day out, always

"WHAT'S HAPPENED TO ME?" HE THOUGHT. IT WAS NO DREAM.

on the road. The stress of sales is much harder than the work going on at the head office, and on top of that I have to cope with the problems of traveling: the worries about train connections, the irregular and bad food, the never-ending stream of new people with whom you never get to make a real connection. To hell with it all!" He felt a slight itching on the top of his back, between his shoulders. He slowly wriggled closer to the bedpost so that he could lift his head more easily, found the itchy part, which was entirely covered with small white spots—he did not know what to make of them and wanted to feel the place with a claw. But he retracted it immediately, for the contact felt like a cold shower all over him.

He slid back again into his previous position. "This getting up early," he thought, for his thoughts were already becoming quite feline, "makes a man stupid. A man must have his sleep. *Other* traveling salesmen live like harem women. For instance, when I go back to my inn during the course of a morning to write up the sales invoices, the other gentlemen are just sitting down to breakfast. If I were to try that with my boss, I'd be fired on the spot. Still—who knows whether that mightn't be good for me, really? If I weren't keeping this job for my parents' sake, I'd have quit ages ago. I would've gone to the boss and told him just what I think from the bottom of my heart. He would've fallen right off his desk! And how bizarre it is, anyway, for him to sit up at that desk and talk down to the employees from way up there, particularly since the chief has trouble hearing, so we have to step up quite close to him. Anyway, I haven't completely given up that hope yet. Once I've made enough money to pay off my parents' debt to him—that should take another five or six years—I'll do it for sure. Then I'll make my big break. In any case, right now I have to get up. My train leaves at five o'clock."

He looked over at the alarm clock ticking away by the chest of drawers. "Good God!" he thought. It was half past six, and the hands were ticking quietly on; in fact, it was *past* the half hour, already nearly quarter to. Could the alarm have failed to ring? No, he saw from the bed that it was properly set for four o'clock; certainly it had rung. Yes, but how could he have slept through that noise, which made the furniture shake? Now, it's true he'd not slept quietly, but evidently he'd slept all the more deeply. Still, what should he do now? The next train left at seven o'clock. To catch that one, he would have to go in a mad rush. The sample collection wasn't packed up yet, and he really didn't feel particularly energetic. And even if he caught the train, there was no avoiding a blowup with the chief, because the firm's errand boy—the boss's minion, really, lacking any backbone or intelligence—would've waited for the five o'clock train and long ago reported the news of his absence. Well then, what if he reported in sick? But that would be extremely embarrassing and suspicious, because during his five years' service Gregor hadn't stayed home sick even once. The boss would certainly come with the doctor from the health insurance company, would reproach his parents for their lazy son and cut short all objections, echoing the insurance doctor's avowed opinion that everyone was always healthy, just lazy about work. And would the doctor in this case be totally wrong? Apart from a really excessive drowsiness after the long sleep, Gregor in fact felt quite well and even had a very strong appetite.

As he was thinking all this over urgently, yet still unable to make the decision to get out of bed—the alarm clock read exactly quarter to seven—there was a cautious knock on the door by the head of the bed.

"Gregor," a voice called—it was his mother!—"it's quarter to seven. Don't you want to be on your way?" Her soft voice! Gregor began to answer but was startled when he heard his own voice: It was clearly and unmistakably his own, but in it was intermingled, as if from below, an irrepressibly pert and endearing squeaking, which left the words distinct only for an instant and distorted them in the reverberation, so that one didn't know if one had heard correctly. Gregor wanted to answer in detail and explain everything, but in these circumstances he confined himself to saying, "Yes, yes, thank you, Mother. I'm getting up right away."

Because of the wooden door the change in Gregor's voice was not really noticeable outside, so his mother calmed down with this explanation and shuffled off. However, as a result of the short conversation, the other family members became aware that Gregor was unexpectedly still at home, and now his father was knocking on one side door, weakly but with his fist. "Gregor, Gregor," he called out, "what's going on?" And, after a short while, he yelled again in a deeper voice: "Gregor! Gregor!" At the other side door, however, his sister knocked lightly. "Gregor? Are you all right? Do you need anything?" Gregor directed answers in both directions: "I'll be ready right away." He made an effort with the most careful articulation and by inserting long pauses between the individual words to remove everything mewling and kittenish from his voice. His father turned back to his breakfast. However, his sister whispered, "Gregor, open the door—I beg you." Gregor had no intention of opening the door; he congratulated himself on maintaining his wise travel habit of locking all doors during the night, even at home.

First he wanted to stand up quietly and undisturbed, get dressed, above all have breakfast, and only then consider further action, for—he realized clearly—by thinking things over in bed he would not reach a reasonable conclusion. Yet the bed seemed warmer and more comfortable than ever, and he was loath to leave it. He felt a strong desire to knead the coverlet with his white paws. But Gregor remembered that he had often in the past felt some light pain or other in bed, perhaps the result of an awkward reclining position, which later turned out to be purely imaginary when he stood up, and he was eager to see how his present fantasies would gradually dissipate. Surely the change in his voice was nothing other than the onset of a real chill, an occupational illness of commercial travelers; of that he had not the slightest doubt.

It was easy to throw aside the blanket. He needed only to push himself up a little, and it fell off by itself. But to continue was difficult, particularly because he was so unusually fat and cuddly. He needed arms and hands to push himself upright. Instead of these, however, he had only four large, soft paws that were incessantly moving with unfamiliar motions, flexing and curling, extending claws and retracting them, and that, in addition, he was unable to control. If he wanted to bend one of them, then it was the first to straighten itself, and if he finally succeeded doing what he wanted with this limb, in the meantime all the others, as if left free, moved around in an excessively darling agitation. "But I must not stay in bed uselessly," said Gregor to himself.

At first he wanted to get out of bed with the lower part of his body, but this lower part—which, by the way, he had not yet looked at and which he also couldn't picture clearly—proved itself too difficult to move, particularly with what felt like a long, bushy tail added to the equation. The attempt went so slowly. When, having become almost frantic, he finally hurled himself forward with all his force and without caution, he chose his direction incorrectly, and he hit the lower bedpost hard. The violent pain that ensued revealed to him that the lower part of his body was at the moment probably the most sensitive. He could not abide his tail being squashed, most of all. This disaster also revealed to Gregor Samsa that he was quite a *large* kitten, for his upper parts were still curled up sweetly in bed.

So now he tried to get his upper body out of bed first, turning his head carefully toward the edge of the bed. He managed to do this easily, and in spite of its width and wriggly, almost liquid weight, his body mass at last slowly followed the turning of his head. But as he finally raised his head outside the bed in the open air, he became anxious about moving forward any farther in this manner, for if he allowed himself eventually to fall by this process, it would take a miracle to prevent his head from getting injured. And at all costs he must not lose consciousness right now. He preferred to remain in bed.

After a second effort, he lay there again, sighing as before, and once again he saw his small limbs fighting one another, having discovered on their own some insignificant piece of fluff; all four of his paws batted it between them, as if he had nothing better to do! If anything, this was worse than earlier, and he didn't see any chance of imposing quiet and order on this arbitrary movement. He told himself again that he couldn't possibly remain in bed and that he really should be prepared to sacrifice everything if there was even the slightest hope of getting himself out of bed in the process. At the same moment, however, he didn't forget to remind himself of the fact that calm—indeed the calmest—reflection—indeed, perhaps a nap—might be better than the most confused decisions. But no! He forced himself to remain sharply awake. Looking for motivation, he directed his gaze as precisely as he could toward the window, but unfortunately there was little confident cheer to be had from a glance at the morning mist, which concealed even the other side of the narrow street. "It's already seven o'clock," he told himself as the alarm clock struck again, "already seven o'clock and still such a fog." And for a little while longer he lay quietly, just purring, struggling valiantly against the onslaught of the nap, as if perhaps waiting for normal and natural conditions to reemerge from the complete stillness.

But then he said to himself, "Before it strikes a quarter past seven, whatever happens I must be completely out of bed. Besides, by then someone from the office will arrive to inquire

about me, because the office will open before seven o'clock."
And he made an effort then to slide his entire body length out
of the bed with a uniform motion. If he let himself fall out of
the bed in this way, his head, which in the course of the fall he
intended to lift up sharply, would probably remain uninjured.
His back seemed to be soft and extremely bendable; nothing
would really happen to it as a result of the fall. His greatest reser-
vation was a worry about the loud noise that the fall would
surely create and which presumably would arouse, if not fright,
then at least concern on the other side of all the doors. However, it had to be tried.

As Gregor was in the process of lifting himself half out of
bed—the new method was more of a game than an effort; he
needed only to slide prudently—it struck him how easy all this
would be if someone were to come to his aid. Two strong
people—he thought of his father and the servant girl—would
have been quite sufficient. They would have only had to push
their arms under his arched back to get him out of the bed, to
bend down with their load, and then merely to exercise patience and care that he completed the flip onto the floor, where
his furry little legs would then, he hoped, acquire a purpose.
But, quite apart from the fact that the doors were locked, should
he really call out for help? In spite of all his distress, he was unable to suppress a smile at this idea.

He had already got to the point where, by stretching out his forepaws and hind paws together, he maintained his equilibrium with difficulty, and very soon he would finally have to decide, for in five minutes it would be a quarter past seven. Then there was a ring at the door of the apartment. "That's someone from the office," he told himself, and he almost froze while his small limbs only danced around all the faster. For one moment everything remained still. "They aren't answering the door," Gregor said to himself, caught up in an absurd hope. But of course then, as usual, the servant girl with her firm footstep went to the door and opened it. Gregor needed to hear only the first word of the visitor's greeting to recognize immediately who it was: the office manager himself. Why was Gregor the only one condemned to work in a firm where the slightest lapse immediately attracted the greatest suspicion? Were all the employees, then, collectively, one and all, scoundrels? Among them was there then no truly devoted person who, if he failed to use just a couple of hours one morning for office work, would become sick from pangs of conscience and really be in no state to get out of bed? Was it really not enough to let an apprentice make inquiries, if such questioning was even necessary? Must the manager himself come, and in the process must it be demonstrated to the entire innocent family that the investigation of this suspicious circumstance could be entrusted only to the intelligence of the manager?

And more as a consequence of the excited state in which this idea put Gregor than as a result of an actual decision, he swung himself with all his might out of the bed. There was a loud thud, but not a real crash. The fall was absorbed somewhat by the carpet and, in addition, his back was more elastic than Gregor had thought, and he had landed squarely on all four paws, as perfectly as a gymnast. For that reason the dull noise was not quite so conspicuous. But he had not held up his head with sufficient care and had hit it. He turned his head, irritated and in pain, and rubbed it on the carpet, first his fuzzy cheeks, then his tufted ears. The pleasure of this action was intense, and he kept at it for some time, despite the danger presented by his manager's unexpected appearance. He could not help himself.

"Something has fallen in there," said the manager in the next room on the left. Gregor tried to imagine to himself whether anything similar to what was happening to him today could have also happened at some point to the manager. At least one had to concede the possibility of such a thing. However, as if to give a rough answer to this question, the manager now, with a squeak of his polished boots, took a few determined steps in the next room. From the neighboring room on the right Gregor's sister was whispering to inform him: "Gregor, your manager is here."

"I know," purred Gregor to himself. But he did not dare make his voice loud enough so that his sister could hear.

"Gregor," his father now said from the neighboring room on the left, "your manager has come and is asking why you have not left on the early train. We don't know what we should tell him. Besides, he also wants to speak to you personally. So please open the door. He will be good enough to forgive the mess in your room."

In the middle of all this, the manager called out in a friendly way, "Good morning, Mr. Samsa."

"He is not well," said his mother to the manager, while his father was still talking at the door. "He is not well, sir, believe me. Otherwise how would Gregor miss a train? The boy has nothing in his head except business. I'm almost angry that he never goes out at night. Right now he's been in the city eight days, but he's come home every evening. He sits here with us at the table and reads the newspaper quietly or studies his travel schedules. It's a quite a diversion for him to busy himself with fretwork. For instance, he framed a small picture over the course of two or three evenings. You'd be amazed how pretty it is. It's hanging right inside the room. You'll see it immediately, as soon as Gregor opens the door. Anyway, I'm happy you're here, good sir. By ourselves, we would never have made Gregor open the door. He's so stubborn, and he's certainly not well, although he denied that this morning."

"I'm coming right away," Gregor said slowly and deliberately and didn't move, so as not to lose one word of the conversation.

"My dear lady," his manager was saying, "I cannot explain it to myself in any other way. I hope it is nothing serious. On the other hand, I must also say that we business people, luckily or unluckily, however one looks at it, very often simply have to overcome a slight indisposition for business reasons."

"So can the manager come in to see you now?" asked his father impatiently and knocked once again on the door. "No," said Gregor. In the neighboring room on the left a painful stillness descended. In the neighboring room on the right his sister began to sob.

Why didn't his sister go to the others? She'd probably just gotten up out of bed now and hadn't even started to get dressed yet. Then why was she crying? Because he wasn't getting up and wasn't letting the manager in? Because he was in danger of losing his position, and because then his boss would badger his parents again with the old demands? Those were probably unnecessary worries right now. Gregor was still here and wasn't thinking at all about abandoning his family. At the moment he was lying right there on the carpet, and no one who knew about his condition would've seriously demanded that he let the manager in. But Gregor wouldn't be casually fired right away because of this small discourtesy, for which he would find an easy and suitable excuse later on. It seemed to Gregor that it might be far more reasonable to leave him in peace at the moment, instead of disturbing him with all this crying and conversation. But it was the very uncertainty of the situation that distressed the others and excused their behavior. Quite without noticing he was doing it, Gregor began to wash himself, licking one paw and running it over his long white whiskers repeatedly.

"Mr. Samsa," the manager was now shouting, his voice raised, "what's the matter? You are barricading yourself in your room, answering with only a yes and a no, making serious and unnecessary troubles for your parents, and neglecting—I mention this only incidentally —your professional duties in a truly unheard-of manner. I am speaking here in the name of your parents and your employer, and I am requesting from you in all seriousness an immediate and clear explanation. I am amazed. I am amazed. I thought I knew you as a calm, reasonable person, and now you suddenly appear to want to start parading around in weird moods. The chief indicated to me earlier this very day a possible explanation for your neglect—it concerned the collection of cash entrusted to you a short while ago—but in truth I almost gave him my word of honor that this explanation could not be correct. However, now I see here your unimaginable pigheadedness, and I am totally losing any desire to speak up for you in the slightest. And your position is not at all the most secure. Originally I intended to mention all this to you privately, but since you are letting me waste my time here uselessly, I don't know why the matter shouldn't come to the attention of your parents. Your productivity has also been very unsatisfactory recently. Of course, it's not the time of year to conduct exceptional business, we recognize that, but a time of year for conducting no business? There is no such thing at all, Mr. Samsa, and such a thing must never be."

"But, sir," called Gregor, beside himself and, in his agitation, forgetting everything else, "I'm opening the door immediately, this very moment. A slight indisposition, a dizzy spell, has prevented me from getting up. I'm still lying in bed right now. But I'm quite refreshed once again. I'm in the midst of getting out of bed. Just have patience for a short moment! Things are not going as well as I thought. But I'm all right. How suddenly a thing can overcome someone! Just yesterday everything was fine with me. My parents certainly know that. Actually, yesterday evening I had a small symptom of something. They must have seen that. Why didn't I report that to the office? But we always think we'll get over an illness without having to stay home. Sir, please, don't upset my parents! There is really no basis for these criticisms you're making against me; really, nobody has said a word to me about any of this. Perhaps you haven't seen the latest orders I shipped. In any case, I'll set out on the eight o'clock train; these few hours of rest have helped me feel stronger. There's no need for you to wait, sir— I will be at the office in person right away. Please, say so to the chief and give him my respects!"

While Gregor was quickly blurting all this out, hardly aware of what he was meowing, he found that he had somehow moved close to the chest of drawers without effort, probably as a result of the practice he had already had in bed, and now he was trying to scramble up to the top of it. Actually, he wanted to open the door. He really wanted to let himself be seen by and to speak with the manager; he was keen to find out what they all would say when they saw him. If they were startled, then Gregor had no more responsibility and could be calm. But if they accepted everything quietly, then he would have no reason to get excited and, if he got a move on, could really be at the station around eight o'clock.

At first he slid down a few times on the smooth chest of drawers. But at last he gave himself a final swing and stood upright there. He was no longer at all aware of the pains in his lower body, no matter how they might still sting. Now he let himself fall against the back of a nearby chair, on the edge of

"BUT, SIR," CALLED GREGOR, "I'M OPENING THE DOOR IMMEDIATELY,
THIS VERY MOMENT."

which he braced himself with his striped limbs. By doing this he gained control over himself and kept quiet, for he could now hear the manager.

"Did you understand a single word?" the manager asked his parents. "Is he playing the fool with us?"

"For God's sake," cried his mother, already in tears, "Gregor is never so silly. Perhaps he's very ill and we're upsetting him. Grete! Grete!" she yelled at that point.

"Mother?" called his sister from the other side. They were making themselves understood through Gregor's room.

"You must go to the doctor right away. Gregor is sick. Hurry to the doctor. Have you heard Gregor speak yet?"

"That was an animal's voice," said the manager, remarkably quietly compared to the mother's cries.

"Anna! Anna!" yelled Gregor's father through the hall to the servant girl in the kitchen, clapping his hands. "Fetch a locksmith right away!" The two young women were already running through the hall with swishing skirts—how had his sister dressed herself so quickly?—and yanked open the doors of the apartment. Gregor couldn't hear the doors closing at all. They had probably left them open, as is customary in an apartment where a huge misfortune has taken place.

However, Gregor had become much calmer. All right, people did not understand his words anymore, although they seemed clear enough to him, clearer than previously, perhaps because his ears had gotten used to them. But at least people now understood that things were not all right with him and were prepared to help him. The confidence and assurance with which the first arrangements had been carried out made him feel good. He felt himself included once again in the circle of humanity and was expecting from both the doctor and the locksmith, without differentiating between them with any real precision, splendid and surprising results. In addition, he felt sure that one or the other of them might scratch him behind the ears, or stroke his fur, and he looked forward to that with great anticipation. In order to get as clear a voice as possible for the critical conversation that was imminent, he coughed a little, and certainly took the trouble to do this in a really subdued way, since it was possible that even this noise sounded somewhat different from a human cough. He no longer trusted himself to decide anymore. Meanwhile in the next room it had become really quiet. Perhaps his parents were sitting with the manager at the table whispering; perhaps they were all leaning against the door listening.

Gregor crept slowly toward the door, as if stalking it, with the help of the easy chair, behind which he hid before throwing himself against the door. He held himself upright against it—the balls of his tiny paws had a little sticky stuff on them—

and rested there momentarily from his exertion. Then he made an effort to turn the key in the lock with his mouth. Unfortunately it seemed that he had no real facility with his feline mouth. His rough tongue lapped uselessly at the key, and his kitten-teeth slid off its brass handle. How was he to grab hold of the key? But then he realized that, as if to make up for his tiny teeth, his jaws were naturally very strong; with their help he managed to get the key really moving. He didn't notice that he was obviously inflicting some damage on himself, for a trickle of blood came out of his mouth, flowed over the key, and dripped onto the floor.

"Just listen for a moment," said the manager in the next room. "He's turning the key." For Gregor that was a great encouragement. But they all should've called out to him, including his father and mother. "Come on, Gregor," they should've shouted, "keep going, keep working on the lock." Imagining that all his efforts were being observed with suspense, he bit down frantically on the key with all the force he could muster. As the key turned more, he danced around the lock. Now he was holding himself upright only with his mouth, and to continue turning the key he had to hang onto it and press down on it with the whole weight of his body. The quite distinct click of the lock as it finally snapped really woke Gregor up. Breathing heavily, he said to himself, "So I didn't need the locksmith," and he set his furry brown head against the door handle to open the door completely.

Because he had to open the door in this way, it was already open very wide without him yet being really visible. He first had to turn himself slowly around the edge of the door, very carefully, of course, if he didn't want to fall awkwardly on his back right at the entrance into the room. He was still preoccupied with this difficult movement, and had no time to pay attention to anything else, when he heard the manager exclaim a loud "Oh!"—it sounded like the wind whistling—and now he saw him, nearest to the door, pressing his hand against his open mouth and moving slowly back, as if an invisible constant force was pushing him away. His mother—in spite of the manager's presence she was standing here with her hair sticking up on end, still a mess from the night—was looking at his father with her hands clasped. She then went two steps toward Gregor and collapsed right in the middle of her skirts, which were spread out all around her, her face sunk on her breast, peering at him with large and delighted eyes. She held out her arms and Gregor leapt happily into them, propelled toward her lap by some ancient instinct he could not suppress. His bulk was too great for her to embrace wholly, however, and Gregor wondered at how large he had already grown, so that his mother could scarcely get her arms around his prodigious girth. His father clenched his fist with a hostile expression, as if he wished to push Gregor away from his wife, then looked uncertainly around the living room, covered his eyes with his hands, and cried so that his mighty belly shook.

At this point Gregor did not take one step off his mother's lap, but leaned his body against the firm solidity of her breast, so that only half his body was visible, as well as his head, tilted sideways, with which he peeped over her elbow at the others. Meanwhile it had become much brighter outside. Standing out clearly from the other side of the street was a part of the endless gray-black house situated opposite—it was a hospital—with its severe regular windows breaking up the facade. The rain was still coming down, but only in large individual drops visibly and firmly thrown down one by one onto the ground. The breakfast dishes were standing piled around on the table, because for his father breakfast was the most important meal of the day, which he prolonged for hours by reading various newspapers. Directly across on the opposite wall hung a photograph of Gregor from the time of his military service; it was a picture of him as a lieutenant, smiling and worry free, with his hand on his sword, demanding respect for his bearing and uniform. The door to the hall was ajar, and since the door to the apartment was also open, one could see out into the landing of the apartment and the start of the staircase going down.

"Now," said Gregor, well aware that he was the only one who had kept his composure. "I'll get dressed right away, pack up the collection of samples, and set off. You'll allow me to set out on my way, will you not? You see, sir, I'm not pig-headed, and I am happy to work. Traveling is exhausting, but I couldn't live without it. Where are you going—to the office, yes? Will you report everything fairly? A person can be incapable of work momentarily, but that's precisely the best time to remember his earlier achievements and to consider that later, after the obstacles have been shoved aside, that person will work all the more eagerly and intensely. I am really so indebted to our chief—you know that perfectly well. On the other hand, I'm concerned for the well-being of my parents and my sister. I'm in a fix here, but I'll work myself out of it again. Don't make things more difficult for me than they already are; please, speak up on my behalf in the office! People don't like traveling salesmen; I know that. People think we earn pots of money and thus lead a fine life. They don't have any special reason, I know, to think through this prejudice more carefully. But you, sir, you have a better perspective on what's involved than other people—even, I tell you in total confidence, a better perspective than the chairman himself, who in his capacity as our employer may sometimes make casual misjudgments of an employee. You also know well enough that the traveling salesman, who's

SHE HELD OUT HER ARMS AND GREGOR LEAPT HAPPILY INTO THEM,
PROPELLED BY SOME ANCIENT INSTINCT.

outside the office almost the entire year, can become so easily a victim of gossip, coincidences, and groundless complaints, against which it's impossible for him to defend himself, since for the most part he doesn't hear about them at all, unless it's when he's finally home after finishing a trip, exhausted, and then feels in his bones the nasty consequences, which he can't even trace back to their origins. Please, sir, don't leave without saying something, without telling me you'll at least concede that I'm at least somewhat right!"

But at Gregor's first words the manager had turned away, looking with pursed lips over his twitching shoulders at Gregor. During Gregor's speech he did not stay still for a moment but kept moving away toward the door, painstakingly slowly, without taking his eyes off Gregor, as if trying to escape some secret ban on leaving the room. He now reached the hall, and given the sudden movement with which he finally pulled his foot out of the living room, one could have believed that he had just burned it. There in the hall, he stretched his right hand out toward the staircase, as if some truly supernatural relief awaited him there.

Gregor realized that he must not under any circumstances allow the manager to leave in this frame of mind—especially if his position in the firm was not to be placed in the greatest danger. His parents did not understand all this very well. Over the long years, they had developed the conviction that Gregor was set for life in his firm, and, in addition, they had so many immediate troubles to worry about nowadays that they'd been unable to spare a thought for the future. But Gregor did have such foresight. The manager must be held back, calmed down, convinced, and ultimately won over. The future of Gregor and his family truly depended on it! Oh, if only his sister would show her face! She was clever. She had already giggled while Gregor was still lying quietly on his belly, purring, and Gregor expected this meant he had one ally, at least. The manager, who was fond of the ladies, would certainly let himself be guided by her. She would have closed the door to the apartment and talked the man out of his fright in the hall. But his sister did not come rescue him. Gregor must deal with it himself.

Forgetting that he still didn't know much about his present ability to move and that his speech possibly—indeed, probably—had once again not been understood, Gregor pushed back out of his mother's embrace, intending to approach the manager, who was already holding tight onto the handrail with both hands on the landing in a ridiculous way. But as Gregor looked for something against which he could hold himself upright, with a small yowl he scrabbled and immediately fell down onto his four little legs. Scarcely had this happened when he felt for the first time that morning a general physical well-being. His small limbs had firm, thickly carpeted floor under them; they obeyed perfectly, as he noticed to his joy, and strove to carry him forward in the direction he wanted. Right away he believed that the final relief from all his suffering was at hand. But at that very moment, as he lay on the floor kneading the carpet in a restrained manner quite close to his mother, who had apparently forgotten her initial delight at the appearance of a large kitten in place of a son, she suddenly sprang right up with her arms spread far apart and her fingers extended, crying out, "Help, for God's sake, help!" She held her head bowed down, as if she wanted to view Gregor better, but ran senselessly back, contradicting that gesture, forgetting that behind her stood the table with all the dishes on it. When she reached the table, she sat down heavily on it, as if absent-mindedly, and did not appear to notice at all that next to her coffee was pouring out onto the carpet in a full stream from the large overturned container.

"Mother, Mother," said Gregor quietly, looking over toward her. He suddenly felt desperate to be in her lap once more, to have her stroke his head, and pet him, and perhaps give him a bit of fish. But she would not look at him. The manager momentarily disappeared completely from his mind. At the sight of the flowing coffee Gregor couldn't stop himself licking his chops a few times. At that his mother screamed all over again, hurried from the table, and collapsed into the arms of his father as he rushed toward her. But Gregor had no time right now for his parents—the manager was already on the staircase. His chin level with the banister, the manager looked back for the last time. Gregor took an initial movement to catch up to him if possible. But the manager must have suspected something, because he made a leap down over a few stairs and disappeared, shouting "Huh!" along the way. The sound echoed back up through the stairwell.

The manager's flight seemed to agitate Gregor's father, who earlier had been relatively calm. Unfortunately, instead of running after the man—or at least not hindering Gregor from his pursuit—with his right hand he grabbed hold of the manager's cane, which he had left behind along with his hat and overcoat on a chair. With his left hand, his father picked up a large newspaper from the table, and, stamping his feet on the floor, he set out to drive Gregor back into his room by waving the cane and the newspaper. No plea of Gregor's was of any use; no plea could even be understood. No matter how willing he was to turn his head respectfully, his father just stomped all the harder with his feet. The newspaper waved frighteningly in his vision, filling him with a curious terror, that he might be beaten with the news of the day, or worse.

Across the room his mother had pulled open a window, in

spite of the cool weather; leaning out with her hands on her cheeks, she pushed her face far outside the window. Between the alley and the stairwell a strong draft came up, the curtains on the window flew around, the newspapers on the table swirled about, and individual sheets fluttered down over the floor. His father relentlessly pressed forward, hissing furiously like a wild man. Now, Gregor had no practice at all in bolting away—and this backing up through the half-open door was really very slow going. If Gregor had only been allowed to take his own time about it, he would have been in his room presently, but he was afraid to make his father impatient by the time-consuming process of deciding whether he wished to be inside or outside a door—for such things seemed to take much longer to work their way through his feline brain than they once had—and each moment he faced the threat of a mortal blow on his head or back from the cane in his father's hand. Finally Gregor had no other option, for he noticed with horror that he did not yet understand how to maintain his attention on one thing when he desired so many things at once. And so he began, amid constant anxious sideways glances in his father's direction, to turn himself around as quickly as possible, although in truth this was only done at a leisurely, unconcerned pace that any man might find infuriating. But Gregor found himself unable to move any other way. Perhaps his father noticed his good intentions, for he did not disrupt Gregor in this motion, but with the tip of the cane like a pointer he even directed Gregor's sauntering movement here and there.

If only his father would not hiss so unbearably! Because of that Gregor totally lost his head. He was already almost within his own room, when, with this hissing constantly in his ear, he just couldn't help turning back a little, to hiss in return, as a cat's honor demanded. Gregor did so, and immediately regretted it. He'd been successful in squeezing partway through the half-open door, but now it became clear that his body was too wide to go through any farther. He had already grown quite alarmingly huge and rotund, larger and furrier than any reasonable person might expect a kitten of only a few hours' age, or indeed an adult cat of any description. Naturally his father, in his present mental state, had no idea of opening the door wider to create a comfortable passage for Gregor to get through. His single fixed thought was that Gregor must get into his room as *quickly* as possible. He would never have allowed the elaborate preparations that Gregor required to consider the door, consider himself, groom his whiskers, rub his cheeks against the jamb, further consider the nature of both doors and salesmen, and finally sniff at the air of his room, to see if it offered suitable napping opportunities, and thus perhaps, at the end of it all, get through the door. On the contrary, as if there were no obstacle and with a peculiar noise, he now forced Gregor forward. Behind Gregor, the sound at this point was no longer like the voice of just one man. Now it was truly no joke, and Gregor forced himself, come what might, into the door.

The left side of his velvety, chubby body was lifted up. He lay at an angle in the door opening. His one flank was sore from the scraping. On the white door bits of fur were left clinging. Soon he was stuck fast and could not move anymore on his own. The white paws on his left hung twitching in the air above, and the right ones were pushed painfully into the floor. Then his father gave him one really strong liberating push from behind, and he sprang, his pride wounded severely, far into the interior of his room. The door was slammed shut with the cane, and finally it was quiet.

# II.

G regor woke from a heavy sleep in the evening twilight. He would certainly have woken up soon in any case, for he felt well rested and wide awake, but it seemed to him that, in fact, it had been a hurried step and a cautious closing of his door that had aroused him.

Light from the electric streetlamps outside lay pale here and there on the ceiling and on the higher parts of the furniture, but on the floor, around Gregor, it was dark. He pushed himself slowly toward the door, his whiskers twitching, which he now learned to value for the first time, for they allowed him to check what was happening out there in the shadows. His entire left side felt like one long unpleasantly stretched scar, and he really had to hobble on his three good legs, because, in addition, one poor paw had been seriously wounded in the course of the morning incident—it was almost a miracle that only one had been hurt!—and dragged lifelessly behind.

By the door he spotted that which had enticed him into motion: the smell of something to eat. A bowl stood there, filled with milk, in which swam tiny pieces of white bread. He almost laughed with joy, for his hunger now was much greater than it had been in the morning, and he immediately plunged half his face into the milk. But he soon drew it back again, because it was difficult for him to eat on account of his delicate left side— he could eat only if his entire body was comfortable, which it presently was not. He turned away from the bowl sadly and crept back into the middle of the room.

In the living room, as Gregor saw through the crack in the door, the gas was lit, but where, on other occasions at this time of day, his father was accustomed to read the afternoon newspaper in a loud voice to his mother and sometimes also to his sister, at the moment no sound was audible. Now, perhaps this reading aloud—which he had never been home to see himself, but of which his sister had always told him—had recently fallen out of their general routine. But everything was so *still*, despite that the apartment was certainly not empty. "What a quiet life the family leads," Gregor said to himself, and as he stared ahead into the darkness, he felt a great pride that he had been able to provide such a life in a beautiful apartment like this for his parents and his sister. But what if, now, all tranquility, all prosperity, all contentment was to come to a horrible end? In order not to lose himself in such thoughts, Gregor preferred to set himself moving, so he bent and began to thoroughly lick his hind leg in the middle of his room.

Once during the course of the long evening, one side door—and then the other door—opened just a tiny crack and quickly closed again. Someone presumably had wanted to come in but had then thought better of it. Gregor immediately took up a position by the living room door, determined to bring in the hesitant visitor somehow or other or at least to find out who it might be. But he waited in vain; the door was not opened again. Earlier, when the door had been locked, they had all wanted to come in to him; now, when he had opened one door and when the others had obviously been opened during the day, no one came anymore, and the keys were stuck in the locks on the outside.

The light in the living room was turned off only late at night, and now it was easy to establish that his parents and his sister had stayed awake all this time, for one could hear clearly as all three moved away on tiptoe. So now it was certain that no one would come into Gregor anymore until the morning.

Thus, he had a long time to think undisturbed about how he should reorganize his life from scratch. There in the high, open room, he felt compelled by some unknown instinct to crouch on the floor, his haunches drawn up and his paws tucked under his white, fluffy chest. He purred deeply, and yet the room made him anxious, without his being able to figure out the reason, for he had lived there for five years. With a sudden, half-unconscious springing to action, but not without a bit of shame, he scurried under the couch, where, in spite of the fact that his back was a little cramped and he could no longer lift up his head, he felt very comfortable.

There he remained the entire night, which he spent partly in a state of semi-sleep, out of which his hunger constantly woke him with a start, but partly in a state of worry and murky hopes, which all led to the conclusion that for the time being he would have to keep calm and—with patience and the greatest consideration for his family—tolerate the troubles that in his present condition he was now forced to cause them.

EARLY IN THE MORNING—scarcely past night, really—Gregor had an opportunity to test the power of the decisions he had just made, for his sister Grete, almost fully dressed, opened the door from the hall into his room and looked eagerly inside. She did not find him immediately, but when she noticed him under the couch—God, he had to be *somewhere* or other, for he could hardly fly away!—she got such a shock that, without being able to control herself, she slammed the door shut once again from the outside. However, as if she was sorry for her behavior, she immediately opened the door again and walked in on her tiptoes, as if she was creeping up upon someone and wishing to pounce upon them. Gregor had pushed his head forward just to the edge of the couch to look at her when she exclaimed and fell upon him, gathering up his bulk into her arms, and all in secret nuzzling and speaking sweetly to him. Yet he could not enjoy her attentions, which in any event were far too familiar for his taste. He was too hungry to be petted and fawned over thus. Would she not notice that he had left the milk standing, not indeed from any lack of hunger, that it was now warm and stale, and would she bring in something else for him to eat? Something like meat, wet and soft, as his heart truly desired? If she did not do it on her own, he would sooner starve to death than call her attention to the fact, although he had a really powerful urge to claw free and abase himself at his sister's feet, and beg her for something or other good and juicy to eat.

Finally his sister ceased cuddling his large white paws, which he endured most patiently, and noticed with astonishment that the bowl was still full, with only a little milk spilled around it. She set him on the couch and picked it up immediately, although not with her bare hands but with a rag, and took it out of the room. Gregor immediately began imagining what she would bring next—but he never could have predicted what his sister, out of the goodness of her heart, in fact did. She brought him, to test his taste, an *entire selection*, all spread out on an old newspaper. There were shredded bits of liver left over from breakfast; chicken still on the bone from the evening meal, smeared with a white sauce; some raisins and almonds; kippers that Gregor had declared inedible two days earlier; a slice of dry bread; and a slice of salted bread smeared with butter. In addition to all this, she put down a bowl—which Gregor supposed had been designated as his alone—into which she had poured some water. And out of her delicacy of feeling, since she knew that he would not eat in front of her, she went away very quickly and even turned the key in the lock, so that Gregor would understand that he could make himself as comfortable as he wished. Gregor's small limbs quivered: The time for eating had come! His wounds must, in any case, have healed overnight; he felt no handicap on that score. He was astonished at that and thought about how more than a month ago he had cut his finger slightly with a knife and how this wound had still hurt even the day before yesterday.

"Am I now going to be less sensitive," he thought, already sucking greedily on the kippers, which had strongly attracted him right away, more than all the other foods. Quickly and with his eyes watering with satisfaction, he ate one after the other: the liver, the chicken, and the sauce. The bread and fruit, by contrast, didn't taste good to him. He couldn't bear the smell and even carried the things he wanted to eat a little distance away. By the time his sister slowly turned the key as a sign that he should withdraw, he was long finished and now lay lazily in the same spot. The noise immediately startled him, despite that he was already almost asleep, and he scurried back again under the couch. But it cost him great self-control to remain under the couch, even for the short time his sister was in the room, because his body had filled out somewhat on account of the rich meal, and in the narrow space there he could scarcely breathe. Amid minor attacks of asphyxiation, he looked at her with somewhat protruding, limpid eyes, as his unsuspecting sister swept up with a broom not just the remnants, but even the foods that Gregor had not touched at all, as if these were also now useless, and as she dumped everything quickly into a bucket, which she closed with a wooden lid, and then carried all of it out of the room. She had hardly turned around before Gregor had already dragged himself out from the couch, stretched out, and let his body expand.

IN THIS WAY Gregor got his food every day: once in the morning, when his parents and the servant girl were still asleep, and a second time after the common noon meal, for his parents were, as before, asleep then for a little while, and the servant girl was sent off by his sister on some errand or other. They certainly would not have wanted Gregor to starve to death, but perhaps they could not have endured finding out what he ate other than by hearsay. Perhaps his sister wanted to spare them what was possibly only a small grief, for they were really suffering quite enough already.

What sorts of excuses people had used on that first morning to get the doctor and the locksmith out of the house Gregor was completely unable to ascertain. Since they could not understand him, no one, not even his sister, thought that he might be able to understand others, and thus, when his sister was in her room, he had to be content with listening now and then to her sighs and invocations to the saints, her occasional kissing, smacking sounds, meant to entice him to her lap. Only later, when she had grown somewhat accustomed to everything—naturally there could never be any talk of her growing *completely* accustomed to it—Gregor sometimes caught a comment that sounded almost as though the situation were normal and no source of alarm. "Well, today it tasted good to him," she said, if Gregor had really cleaned his plate; whereas, on the other hand, when she insisted (as she did with increasing frequency) on bringing him bread and vegetables, cakes, candies and other unappetizing foodstuffs that were not fish or other soft meats, or even the milk he had been too injured to enjoy fully, his sister would say sadly, "Now everything has stopped again."

But while Gregor could get no new information directly, he did hear a good deal from the room next door, and as soon as he heard voices, he would scurry right away to the appropriate door and press his entire body against it, purring and rubbing his cheek against the grain of the wood in a fashion he found most embarrassing yet a distinct source of pleasure. In the early days especially, there was no conversation that was not concerned with him in some way or other, even if only in secret. For two days, all the family's meal-time discussions he could hear were about how people should now behave toward him; but they also talked about the same subject in the times between meals, for there were always at least two family members at home, since no one really wanted to remain there alone with him and they could not under any circumstances imagine leaving the apartment completely empty. In addition, on the very first day the servant girl—it was not completely clear what and how much she knew about what had happened—on her knees had begged his mother to let her go immediately, and when she said goodbye about fifteen minutes later, she thanked them for the dismissal with tears in her eyes, as if she was receiving the greatest favor that people had shown her there, and, without anyone demanding it from her, she swore a fearful oath not to betray anyone, not even the slightest bit, if they would only allow her to stroke Gregor's large, striped head just once, which she found adorable, yet terrifying.

Gregor endured this imposition as stoically as he was able; no others witnessed it, a fact for which he was glad, and again, he found that purring which he could neither control nor predict, rumbling up from his furry chest, even now growing broader and more stately.

Now his sister had to team up with his mother to do the cooking, although that didn't create much trouble because people were eating almost nothing. Again and again Gregor listened as one of them vainly invited another one to eat and received no answer other than, "Thank you. I've had enough," or something like that. And perhaps they had stopped having anything to drink, too. His sister often asked his father whether he wanted to have a beer and gladly offered to fetch it herself, and when his father was silent, she said, in order to remove any reservations he might have, that she could send the caretaker's wife to get it. But then his father finally uttered a resounding "No," and nothing more would be spoken about it.

ON THE FIRST DAY of Gregor's changed situation, his father had laid out all the financial circumstances and prospects to his mother and sister. From time to time since, the elder Mr. Samsa would stand up from the table, take the small lockbox salvaged from his business, which had collapsed five years previously, and pull out some document or notebook. (Gregor could hear the distinct sound of the box's complicated lock opening and, after his father was done with it, closing and locking again.) These explanations by his father were the first somewhat enjoyable thing that Gregor had the chance to listen to since his imprisonment. Gregor had thought that no money at *all* remained from that business; at least, his father had told him nothing to contradict that view, and Gregor in any case hadn't asked him about it. At the time, Gregor's only concern had been to work as hard as he possibly could so that his family might forget as quickly as possible the financial misfortune that had brought them all into such a state of complete hopelessness. And so at that point he'd applied himself to his job with a special intensity and from an assistant had become, almost overnight, a traveling salesman, which naturally opened entirely different possibilities for earning money, as his successes at work were turned immediately into cash commissions, which could be brought home and set on the table in front of his astonished and delighted family.

Those had been beautiful days, and they had never come back afterward, at least not with the same splendor, despite that Gregor later earned so much money that he was in a position to bear the expenses of the entire family, which was precisely what he did. They had become quite accustomed to it, both the family and Gregor as well. They took the money with thanks, and he happily surrendered it—but as that arrangement continued, their warm family intimacy faded. Only Grete remained still close to Gregor, and it was his secret plan to send her next year to the conservatory, regardless of the great expense that necessarily involved and which would have to be made up in other ways. Unlike Gregor, she loved music very much and knew how to play the violin charmingly. Now and then during Gregor's short stays at home, music school would come up in conversations with his sister, but always only as a beautiful dream whose realization was unimaginable, and their parents never listened to these innocent expectations with pleasure. But Gregor dwelled upon it with scrupulous consideration and intended to present his plan to Grete and his parents ceremoniously on Christmas.

In his present situation, he would recall such thoughts, recognizing their futility now, as he pushed himself right up against the door and listened to the others. Sometimes, in his general exhaustion, he couldn't listen anymore and let his head droop sleepily against the door, but he immediately pulled himself together, for even the small sound he made by this motion was heard outside and caused everyone to immediately fall silent. "There he goes again," his father said after a while, clearly turning toward the door, and only then would the interrupted conversation gradually be resumed again.

Gregor found out clearly enough—for his father tended to repeat himself often in his explanations, partly because he had not concerned himself with these matters for a long time now, and partly also because his mother did not understand everything right away the first time—that, in spite of all the bad luck they'd suffered, a modest sum of money was still available from the old times, and the interest, which had not been touched, had in the intervening time gradually increased a bit. In addition, the money that Gregor had brought home every month—he had kept only a few florins for himself—had not been completely spent and had grown into a small capital amount. Gregor, behind his door, nodded eagerly, rejoicing over this unanticipated foresight and frugality. He even allowed himself a small, triumphant squeak, which he prayed went unheard. True, had he known of this excess money, he could have paid off more of his father's debt to his employer, and the day on which he could be rid of his horrid job would have been a lot closer—but now things were doubtlessly better the way his father had arranged them.

At the moment, however, this savings was not nearly enough to permit the family to live on the interest payments. Perhaps it would be enough to maintain them for a year or two at most, but that was all. Thus, it should ideally continue to be set aside for use as a last resort, in case of a true emergency; meanwhile, the money to live on would have to be earned. Now, Gregor's father was old, and though he was a healthy man, he had not worked at all for five years and thus could not be counted on for very much. He had, in those five years—the first time off he'd ever had in his trouble-filled but unsuccessful life—put on a good deal of fat. And should Gregor's old mother now work for money, a woman who suffered from asthma, exacerbated now by Gregor's constant shedding of his fine fur and dander; a woman for whom just wandering through the apartment was a great strain, who spent every second day on the sofa by the open window laboring for breath? Or should his sister go to work to earn money, a girl who was still a seventeen-year-old child whose earlier lifestyle had been so very delightful that it had consisted of dressing herself nicely, sleeping in late, helping around the house, taking part in a few modest enjoyments, and, above all, playing the violin? When the options were laid out like that, Gregor went away from the door and threw himself on the cool leather sofa beside the door, for he was quite hot from shame and sorrow.

Often he lay there all night long. He didn't get a minute of sleep, just scratched on the leather for hours at a time. Finally, recalling the satisfaction that the sight of the street outside used to bring him, he undertook the difficult task of shoving a chair over to the window; then he crept up on the windowsill and, braced in the chair, leaned against the glass to look out.

With each passing day, Gregor found that he could see things with more and more clarity, even things a long distance away, especially in the dark: the hospital across the street, the all-too-frequent sight of which he had previously cursed, was visible clearly now, even to the colors of the beards of various patients, and if he had not been precisely aware that he lived in the quiet but completely urban Charlotte Street, he could have believed that from his window he was peering out at an aston-ishing painting, in which the clear heaven and the teeming earth had merged and were full of extraordinarily sharply drawn scenes and landscapes. His attentive sister must have observed a couple of times that the chair stood by the window, for there-after, upon cleaning up the room, she made sure to push the chair back right against the window, and from now on she even left the inner casement open.

If Gregor had only been able to speak to his sister and thank her for everything that she had to do for him, he could have tolerated her attentions more easily. Grete sought to cover up the awkwardness of everything as much as possible—particularly that of cleaning up his business, which was now messier than it once was. As time went by, she naturally got more successful at it. But with the passing of time, Gregor also came to understand everything more precisely. Even her entrance was terrible for him. As soon as she entered, she ran straight to him, squealing with delight and chasing him about the room, caring little whether he wished to be held or cosseted. She would shut the window, out of which he spent the better part of his time gazing, and shut the door so that he was quite trapped. She then set to her ministrations, winding her fingers in his long, bushy tail, scratching his ears, speaking nonsense and lifting him high into the air before producing her silver hairbrush and compelling him to lie uncomfortably upon his back while she brushed his tangled fur until it became quite glossy—a process Gregor found extraordinarily painful and annoying. With this fuss and noise she frightened Gregor twice every day, and thus the entire time between her visits he trembled under the couch, though he knew very well that she would certainly have spared him gladly if only he had been a little less handsome, furry, or enticing to the spirit of a young girl.

On one occasion—about a month had gone by since Gregor's transformation, and there was now no particular reason anymore for his sister to be startled at Gregor's appearance—she arrived a little earlier than usual and came upon Gregor as he was still looking out the window, immobile and well positioned to frighten someone. It would not have come as a surprise to Gregor if she had not come in, since his position was preventing her from closing the window immediately, lest he fall out. But she not only stepped inside; she brought in a porcelain washtub, picked him up, and bathed him vigorously, ignoring his caterwauls of protest. A stranger really might have concluded from the expression on his face that Gregor wanted to bite her. Instead, the girl produced a rose-colored collar, with bells and bits of shiny material on it, as well as a large, bright buckle. Gregor's heart quailed against the thing, but he could not resist his sister with any effectiveness as she seized his damp scruff and wrangled him into the thing with no ceremony whatsoever.

Of course, when it was done, Gregor immediately concealed himself under the couch and began frantically licking himself to remove any memory of the bath, any thought of the hideous collar, and he had to wait until the noon meal before Grete returned, though she seemed calmer than usual. From this he realized that his appearance was still constantly tempting to her and must remain tempting in future, and that she really had to exert a lot of self-control not to run toward the

SHE BATHED HIM VIGOROUSLY, IGNORING HIS CATERWAULS OF PROTEST.

slightest glimpse of even only that small part of his body which stuck out from under the couch. In order to spare himself, one day Gregor pulled the sheet onto his back and dragged it onto the couch—this task took him four hours—and arranged it in such a way that he was now completely concealed, so his sister, even if she bent down, could not see him. Of course she could remove it, but she left the sheet just as it was, catching his meaning, and Gregor believed he even caught a look of sorrow when, on one occasion, he carefully lifted up the sheet a little with his head to check, as his sister took stock of the new arrangement.

IN THE FIRST two weeks his parents could not bring themselves to visit him, and he often heard how thankfully they acknowledged his sister's present work—whereas, before, they had often grown annoyed at her because she had seemed to them a somewhat useless young woman. However, now both his father and his mother often waited in front of Gregor's door while his sister cleaned up inside and fussed over him, and as soon as she came out, she had to explain in detail how things looked in the room, what Gregor had eaten, how he had behaved this time, and whether perhaps a slight improvement in the direction of his old self was perceptible. In any event, before long his mother wanted to visit Gregor as well, but his father and his sister restrained her, at first with reasons that Gregor listened to very attentively and that he completely endorsed. Later, however, they had to hold her back forcefully, and when she then cried, "Let me go to Gregor. He's my poor son! Don't you understand that I have to go to him?" Gregor then thought that perhaps it would be a good thing if his mother came in— not every day, of course, but maybe once a week. She understood everything much better than his sister, who, in spite of all her courage, was still a child and, in the last analysis, had perhaps undertaken such a task out of childish desire. His mother would surely sit calmly and read while he crouched near her—but not too near. She might reach out and pat him once an hour, if she liked, but she would not importune him in the same way that Grete did, he felt certain.

Gregor's wish to see his mother was soon realized. While during the day he wanted nothing more than to sit himself by the window, he couldn't crawl around very much on the few square inches of the sill. He found it difficult to bear lying quietly during the night, for his paws, his whiskers, his tail all wished to prowl and to hunt—though all that he could find to expend his desire upon was a few dust-motes his sister had missed in her cleaning. Soon eating no longer gave him much pleasure, for the food lay there dead and did not offer any sport at all. So for diversion he acquired the habit of scampering back and forth across the mantel and bookshelves. He was especially fond of hanging from the draperies. The experience was quite different from lying on the floor. It was easier to breathe, a slight vibration went through his body, and in the midst of the almost happy amusement that Gregor found up there, it could happen that, to his own surprise, he let go and hit the floor. However, now he naturally controlled his body quite differently, and he did not injure himself in such a great fall, but without fail landed firmly upon his four paws. His sister noticed immediately the new amusement that Gregor had found for himself—for as he crept around he left behind here and there traces of his wispy white fur—and so she got the idea of making Gregor's bouncing around as easy as possible and thus of removing the furniture, which was starting to get quite scratched and ruined by his attention, especially the chest of drawers and the writing desk.

But she was in no position to do this by herself, and she did not dare to ask her father to help. Thus, Grete had no other choice but to involve their mother while their father was absent. Gregor's mother approached his room with cries of excited joy, but she fell silent at the door. Of course, his sister first checked whether everything in the room was in order. Only then did she let his mother walk in. In great haste, Gregor had dragged the sheet down even farther and wrinkled it more; now the whole thing really looked just like a coverlet thrown carelessly over the couch. On this occasion, Gregor held back from spying out from under the sheet—he didn't need to see his mother this time, he was just happy that she had come. "Come on, he's just hiding," said his sister, and evidently led his mother by the hand. Now Gregor listened as the two women struggled to push the heavy old chest of drawers from its position. His sister constantly took on herself the greater part of the work, without listening to the warnings of his mother, who was afraid that she would strain herself. The work lasted a long time; after about a quarter of an hour had gone by, his mother said it would be better if they left the chest of drawers where it was, because, in the first place, it was too heavy—they would not be finished before his father's arrival, and leaving the chest of drawers in the middle of the room would block all Gregor's pathways—but, in the second place, she pointed out, they could not be certain Gregor would be pleased with the removal of the furniture. To her the reverse seemed to be true: the sight of the empty walls pierced her right to the heart. And why should Gregor not feel the same, since he had been accustomed to the room furnishings for a long time? In an empty room, would he not feel himself abandoned?

"And is it not the case," his mother concluded very quietly, almost whispering as if she wished to prevent Gregor, whose exact location she really didn't know, from hearing even the sound of her voice—for she was convinced that he did not understand her words—"and isn't it a fact that by removing the furniture we're showing that we're giving up all hope of improvement, that we're leaving him to his own resources without any consideration? I think it would be best if we tried to keep the room exactly in the condition it was in before, so that, when Gregor returns to us, he finds everything unchanged and can forget the intervening time all the more easily."

As he heard his mother's words, Gregor realized that the lack of all sensible, adult human contact save his sister's cosseting, together with the monotonous life he'd been forced to spend listening to the family through the walls over the course of these two months, must have confused his understanding, because otherwise he couldn't explain to himself how, in all seriousness, he could have been so keen to have his room emptied. Was he really eager to let the warm room, comfortably furnished with pieces he had inherited, be turned into a cavern in which he would, of course, then be able to sun about in all directions without disturbance, but neither leap to and from the bed, nor hang from the curtains, nor send the papers scattering from the writing desk, a practice that brought him much joy? At the same time, if he indulged his new appetites, would they result in a quick and complete forgetting of his human past as well? Was he then at this point already on the verge of forgetting, and was it only the voice of his mother, which he had not heard for a long time, that had aroused him? No, nothing was to be removed—everything must remain. His mother was right: In his condition he could not function without the beneficial influences of his furniture, as a reminder and a call back to his old self. And if the furniture allowed him to carry out his mad romping about all over the place, then there was no harm in that, but rather a great benefit.

But his sister unfortunately thought otherwise. She had grown accustomed, certainly not without justification, so far as the discussion of matters concerning Gregor was concerned, to act as a special authority with more expertise than their parents—and so now their mother's advice was, for his sister, sufficient reason to *insist* on the removal, not only of the chest of drawers and the writing desk, which were the only items she had thought about at first as they were quite spoiled by his pouncing and racing across them, but also of *all* the furniture, with the exception of the indispensable couch. Of course, it was only childish defiance—and possessiveness of her recent very unexpected but hard-earned favorite pet—that led her to this demand.

But perhaps the enthusiastic sensibility of young women of her age also played a role. This feeling sought release at every opportunity, and with it, Gregor thought, perhaps his sister now felt tempted to make Gregor's situation even more terrifying to the family, so that then she would be able to do even more for him than now. For surely none except Grete would ever trust themselves to enter a room in which Gregor ruled the empty walls all by himself. And so she did not let herself be dissuaded by her mother, who in this room seemed agitated and uncertain and finally yielded, helping Grete with all her energy to push the chest of drawers out of the room.

Now, Gregor could do without the chest of drawers if need be, but the writing desk really had to stay. And scarcely had the women left the room with the chest of drawers, groaning as they pushed it, when Gregor stuck his head out from under the sofa to take a look how he could intervene cautiously and with as much consideration as possible. But unfortunately it was his mother who came back into the room first, while Grete had her arms wrapped around the chest of drawers in the next room and was rocking it back and forth by herself, without moving it from its position. His mother was not used to the sight of Gregor, and he realized he might make her ill with her delicate chest and his voluminous fur, so, frightened for her, Gregor scurried backward to the far end of the sofa—but he could not prevent the sheet from moving forward a little. That was enough to catch his mother's attention. She came to a halt, stood still for a moment, and then went back to Grete.

Gregor kept repeating to himself over and over that really

nothing unusual was going on, that only a few pieces of furniture were being rearranged, but he soon had to admit to himself that the movements of the women to and fro, their quiet conversations, and the scratching of the furniture on the floor affected him like a great swollen commotion on all sides, and, so firmly was he pulling in his head and paws and pressing his belly into the floor, he had to tell himself unequivocally that he wouldn't be able to endure all this much longer. They were cleaning out his room, taking away from him everything he cherished; they had already dragged out the chest of drawers in which the fret saw and other tools were kept, and they were now loosening the writing desk that was fixed tight to the floor, the desk on which he, as a business student, a school student, indeed even as an elementary school student, had written out his assignments. At that moment he really didn't have any more time to check the good intentions of the two women, whose existence he had in any case now almost forgotten, because in their exhaustion they were working really silently, and the heavy stumbling of their feet was the only sound to be heard.

And so he wriggled out—the women were just propping themselves up on the writing desk in the next room in order to take a breather—changing the direction of his path four times. He really didn't know what he should rescue first. Then he saw hanging conspicuously on the wall, which was otherwise already empty, the large framed picture of the woman dressed in nothing but fur. He quickly scurried up to it and pawed at the bottom edge of the gilt frame, clinging to it with desperation. By leaping and scrabbling at the frame, he pulled himself up onto the top of the heavy portrait, where he settled himself, though a part of his ample, striped belly and tail spilled over the picture. At least this painting, which Gregor now covered nearly to the woman's shoulders, would now not be taken away. He twisted his head toward the door of the living room to observe the women as they came back in.

They had not allowed themselves very much rest and were coming back right away. Grete had placed her arm around her mother and held her tightly. "So what shall we take next?" Grete said, looking around. Then her glance met Gregor's from the wall. She kept her composure only because her mother was there. She bent her face toward her mother in order to prevent her from looking around, and said, although in a trembling voice and too quickly, "Come, let's go back to the living room for a moment." Grete's purpose was clear to Gregor: She wanted to bring his mother to a safe place and then chase him down from the painting. Well, let her just try! He squatted on his picture and did not hand it over. He would sooner spring into Grete's face.

But Grete's words had immediately made his mother very

uneasy. She turned around, caught sight of the enormous brown shape against the flowered wallpaper, and, before she became truly aware that what she was looking at was Gregor, screamed out in a high-pitched raw voice, "Oh God, oh God!" and fell with outstretched arms, as if she were surrendering everything, onto the couch and lay there motionless, her hands extended to him as if imploring. Gregor felt a terrible urgency in his fluffy chest and moved to jump down—there would be time enough to save the picture—but he was stuck fast on the glass and the gilt and had to tear himself loose forcefully, which made him topple ungracefully from his perch. He then went to his mother immediately, purring and pressing himself desperately against his mother's chest, as he had when a babe, and accepting her hesitant hands on his large, heavy body, grateful and sorry to have caused such chaos in their comfortable home. His mother, for her part, wept unhappily, for nothing remained that anyone could say. But she did stroke him, and she did let him press his cheek against her hand.

"Gregor, you . . . ," cried out his sister with a raised fist and an urgent glare—for he had never nuzzled *her* so willingly. These were the first angry words she had directed at him since his transformation. She ran into the room next door to bring some spirits or other with which she could revive her mother from her fainting spell. Gregor wanted to help as well; he darted after his sister into the next room, as if he could give her some advice, as he used to once upon a time, but then he had to stand there idly behind her while she rummaged about among various small bottles. Still, she was frightened when she turned around. A bottle fell onto the floor and shattered. A splinter of glass wounded Gregor in the face, some corrosive medicine or other dripped over him. He tried to lick his paw and mop it away, but the taste of it was sour and foul. Now, without lingering any longer, Grete took as many small bottles as she could hold and ran with them to her mother. She slammed the door shut with her foot, leaving Gregor stranded. He was now shut off from his mother, who was perhaps near death, thanks to him. He could not open the door, and he did not want to chase away his sister, who of course had to remain with their mother. At this point, he had nothing to do but wait, and overwhelmed with self-reproach and worry, he began to mew pitifully and knead the carpet below the door, turning in circles and climbing upon the fresh, new furniture that stood in the parlor. Finally, in his despair, as the entire room started to spin around him, he fell asleep on a large table.

A short time elapsed. Gregor lay there limply. All around was still. Perhaps that was a good sign. Then there was a ring at the door. At this, caught outside his designated room, Gregor sprang guiltily away, and noting that the parlor window was quite ajar, slipped out in abject humiliation—and yet with a sharp feeling of release, finally feeling the air on his whiskers. He leapt upon the rose trellis and, half-climbing, half-falling, descended to the wet, cold street below.

Grete went to open the door; their father had arrived. Seeing her alarmed appearance, he immediately asked: "What's happened?" Grete replied with a dull voice—evidently she was pressing her face into her father's chest—"Mother fainted, but she's getting better now. Gregor has broken loose."

"Yes, I have expected that," said his father, "I always told you it would happen, but you women never want to listen."

# III.

It was late evening when Gregor landed. The city lay deep in snow. There was nothing to be seen of his old apartments, for mist and darkness surrounded them, and not the faintest glimmer of light showed where the great building stood. Gregor stood on the road leading back to his house for a long time, looking up at what seemed to be a void. The stones of the street pressed painfully against his paws, nothing at all like the plush carpet of his former apartments, and though the rush of traffic assailed his sensitive ears from the roadway beyond the alley, these discomforts were ameliorated by the wonderful smells of old food and scraps of fish that littered the frozen ground, no doubt tossed out from some high window by a soul not weighed down by such predicaments as Gregor currently faced.

Gregor began to investigate the possibilities of the rubbish heaps, amazed at the delicacy of his nose, its ability to discern haddock from cod, its unerring sense of what had gone to rot and what remained good for a cat's stomach—which indeed he already knew would tolerate much a man's would not—and its cheerful performance of many operations at once, not only snuffling out fish but ascertaining what other creatures had visited the alley before him, what sorts of moods they had been in, and whether or not he could expect rain later this evening. When at home, Gregor had not noticed his nose behaving in this manner; he supposed he had been surrounded entirely by familiar things that he had no need to inspect in any great detail. Nor, truly, had his nose had any pressing need to care for him, as Grete had performed most functions of a nose quite admirably.

"How much my life has changed," Gregor thought," and yet how unchanged it has remained at the bottom of it all!" Even as a man among men, he thought, he had long sensed some small dissonance, some infinitesimal maladjustment in his spirit, causing a vague feeling of discomfiture that not even the most pleasant public functions could ease entirely; and even more than that, that sometimes—no, not sometimes, but *very often*—the mere look of some fellow man of his own station, the mere *look* of him would fill Gregor with helpless embarrassment and panic, even with despair. If he were to dig deep into his most shameful thoughts, he would have to admit that he had even looked at his own sister with such detached horror, at how like an insect she went about her daily routines, never seeming to enjoy them or despise them, or indeed to think at all, seeming so wholly different from Gregor himself that he wondered that they could truly be related, so like different species they lived. Even her violin playing, in which he often took some portion of pleasure, would, when he had fallen out of sorts, sound to him like nothing more than a huge insect's legs rubbing together in some arcane attempt at language.

Finding a choice bit of herring in the road, Gregor licked it thoroughly before beginning to slurp it up, and he considered that he had always tried to quiet his feelings of apprehension as best he could. Friends, if he had had any, might have helped him, if he could have found a kindred heart, a true fellow man to divulge his troubles to; yet the source of all his troubles seemed to be that he did not feel he *had* a fellow man, that he, Gregor Samsa, was singular in the world—alien, even—that to no corner of the city or even the continent could he turn to find a sympathetic person who had felt as he had felt, act as he had acted, suffered as he had suffered. Perhaps he had taken the job as a salesman in order to escape those very apartments where he suffocated alongside his family—perhaps, worse still, he had done it in a vain, desperate hope of finding anyone at all in whom he could confide these unformed, unsettling feelings of unbelonging.

True, there had been peaceful times, times in which these sudden fits of melancholy were still not lacking but in which they were accepted with more philosophy, perhaps inducing a certain lethargy and laziness of habit, but nevertheless allowing him to carry on as a somewhat cold, reserved, canny, and calculating—but all things considered, a normal and civilized enough—man. And yet a man he was no longer, and soon, he felt certain, he would no longer be a kitten either, but a cat, full in the belly and strong in the leg, with ears most pointed and capable. Between Grete's care and his occasional, spontaneous, excited careening about his room, he was becoming quite large and strong, and surely this had been a factor in the great frights he continued to give his family. How long would he keep growing? More pressing—how long could he provide food and warmth for himself now that he had escaped his confinement at home? Gregor had no fear that his father's round, angry face would appear out of the upper windows and alert the neighbors to his presence, leading to a recapture and a swift return to his previous miserable circumstances. More likely, they would all be glad to be rid of him, as he could not in his present state serve any purpose to them, neither to pay his father's debt nor to provide the household nor—but Gregor, thinking clearly now, as sharp-eyed animals will when they find themselves in frozen alleys with their supper in question, could not think of another way in which he was of any use to his relations, nor indeed could he think of the smallest fashion in which they were any use to him.

Perhaps, Gregor thought, this new hardness of feeling could be attributed to the fresh exercise of his altered shape. He had often observed that the cats belonging to his neighbors showed no particular warmth or love for their owners, no matter how fine or poor their food and bedding. If those cats wished to claw up a drapery, they did so without considering the expense to be entered in their masters' ledger, nor the swings of the kitchen maid's broom against their backsides, nor anything save their personal desires. Gregor licked the remainder of the herring from his white paw. He had never acted according to his desires alone, but only according to the dicta of his kin, his duty, and that great filial ledger that ruled his life. He had not resented it; but he had to adapt to his current situation, and despite what they had all hoped, his current situation seemed to be permanent. That difference of spirit he had always felt on the inside was now evident on the outside—and perhaps if all this meant to continue, Gregor might be entitled to some portion of the freedom and uncaring disposition he had always found baffling in the feline species before now.

With this sense of purpose then, Gregor raised his tail, fully erect, and strode from the dark alley of his earlier existence.

WHEN GREGOR SAMSA, coming along the alleyway, walked into the open street, he saw that it was raining. It was not raining much.

On the pavement straight in front of him there were many people walking in the various rhythms of city business. Every now and again one would step forward and cross the road. A little girl was holding a tired puppy in her outstretched arms. Two gentlemen were exchanging information of some sort. The one held his hands palms-up, lifting and lowering them in a regular motion, as though he were balancing a weight. Then one caught sight of a lady whose hat was heavily festooned with ribbons, buckles, and flowers. Gregor shuddered, thinking of the collar that even now itched against his neck. He batted at it with a hindpaw, burning with shame. And hurrying past was a young man with a slim walking cane, his left hand, as though paralyzed, pressed flat to his chest at an odd angle. Now and then there came men who were smoking, trailing clouds along ahead of them. Three gentlemen—two holding lightweight overcoats on their up-crooked forearms—several times made a ritual of walking out from the front of the buildings on the opposite edge of the sidewalk, surveying what was afoot there, and then drawing back into the doorway again, talking all the while.

Gregor darted through the gaps between the passers-by. Instantly he was accosted by carriages on delicate high wheels, drawn along by horses with arched necks. As he tumbled this way and that he caught glimpses of people sitting at ease on the upholstered seats, gazing silently at the pedestrians, the ships in the river-yards, the balconies, and the evening sky. It happened that one carriage surged up behind him and overtook another; the horses pressed against each other, and the harness straps hung dangling. The animals tugged at the reins, the carriage barreled forward, swaying side to side as it came up to speed, until the swerve around the first carriage was completed and the horses moved apart again, only their narrow quiet heads inclined toward each other, and poor Gregor, quite soaked in a frozen slushy slurry of muddy water, had achieved transit across a busy street in his middlingly fashionable district of Prague. He congratulated himself, and then bent immediately to licking himself from head to foot, a compulsion he still found humiliating but undeniable, irresistible, as the sensation of the very slightest speck of dirt caused him to descend into a frenzy of washing, and his fur was now laden with quite a bit more than a speck of filth from his adventures.

Gregor felt tired already. The fur of his cheeks was pale as the faded brownish red of his flanks, which had a kind of Moorish pattern to their stripes and spots. The lady by the doorsteps over there, who had up to now been contemplating her shoes, which were quite visible under her tightly drawn skirt, now looked at him. She did so indifferently, with perhaps a bit of scorn or protective instincts toward the supper she was no doubt preparing beyond the lintel frame. Gregor thought perhaps she looked a bit bored as well. "Well," he thought. "If I could tell her the whole story, she would be astonished! She would certainly give me supper, then, and beg me to tell her more! On the street one works so hard at surviving that one is too tired even to enjoy anything at all. But even all that work does not give a kitten the right to be treated lovingly by everyone; on the contrary, a cat is always alone, an utter stranger and rarely even an object of curiosity. And oh, so long as I say 'one' or 'a cat' instead of 'I,' there is nothing to it and one can easily tell the story, even laugh at its twists and turns; but as soon as I admit to myself that it is me, it is Gregor that has been so ruined, I feel a horror, and a weeping within me."

And so Gregor did feel, as the woman left off gazing at him through the freezing rain and withdrew into her rooms without so much as dashing across the road to cuddle him or pat his head or give him warm milk and a pillow to sleep on. Now that he had no chance of such luxuries he certainly found that he missed them. He felt his small shoulders slump and turned away toward yet more streets and alleyways, all as unfamiliar now as a foreign country, for never had he seen them at such a height, nor been so conscious of their smells and prone to their dangers and wholly unable to hail a hansom cab. Indeed, so sensitive was he to all things that he could not help seeing each and every thing he passed wholly, with his whole being, as if he had to assess their danger to his soft and admittedly fuzzy person before he could safely observe something else. And so when soon enough he happened upon a square near the docks, he saw with great clarity two boys were sitting on a harbor wall playing at dice—which might be thrown at him, or one of the boys might pull his ears.

A man—who might have a daughter waiting at home to whom he might wish to give the present of a kitten!—was reading a newspaper on the steps of a monument that seemed to glare down at Gregor with malevolent expression, a hero flourishing his sword on high as if to lord it over himself in particular. A girl, no doubt as enamoured of weak and furry things as Grete herself, was filling her bucket at the fountain. A fruit-seller was lying beside his wares, gazing at the lake. No doubt between the melons he concealed some foul weapon to use against offending strays and thieves. Through the vacant window and door opening of a café, Gregor could see two men quite at the back quaffing down their wine, surely discussing recipes for roast or boiled cat. The proprietor was sitting at a table in front and dozing—but wake him, and see if he would not chase Gregor off with a rolling pin! A barge was silently making for the little harbor, as if borne by invisible mechanisms over the water—water which would drown him as soon as sparkle in the moonlight. A man in a blue blouse climbed ashore and lashed the line to the pier. Behind the boatman two other beefy men in dark coats with silver buttons carried a bier, on which, beneath a silk cloth, a body lay. But Gregor was not convinced—perhaps even the corpse had designs on him. In ancient Aegypt, did they not bury live cats along with the dead?

And then he saw, near the monument, above which the moon was starting to rise into just the right position to seem to be pierced by the tip of the hero's sword like a large balloon, lounged a large cat not unlike himself—a tabby with long, bold stripes and a languorous expression similar to his father's after a beef dinner and a measure of brandy.

Nobody on the quay took any notice of the reclining cat, nor of the newcomer, as Gregor trotted past the men in black coats who set down the bier and mopped their foreheads, waiting for the boatman. Nobody went near him, nor the tabby;

NEAR THE MONUMENT LOUNGED A LARGE CAT NOT UNLIKE HIMSELF—
A TABBY WITH A LANGUOROUS EXPRESSION.

nobody spared them an inquisitive glance.

It occurred to Gregor that though he could not communicate with Grete or his mother, though his imprecations to his supervisor and his father had sounded even to his own ear like nothing more than a series of tinny squeaks and trills, perhaps those very squeaks and trills would allow him to communicate with that fine tabby gentleman—for the nation of cats was certainly his new family, and if he had any hope of achieving some standing in that household, he ought to begin sooner rather than later his career.

Now Gregor had seen among his neighbors' animals the way in which cats were accustomed to greeting each other: First the beasts hung warily back, then made their approach, sniffing hesitantly at the nose, the whiskers, and sometimes at the nether quarters—he did not feel he could masquerade any enthusiasm for that act with much success—and then, depending on some invisible pheromone indicating accord or total war, either hiss and arch the back in preparation for the attack or purr and nuzzle, rubbing pelts one against the other with apparent pleasure and agreeable satisfaction. Going over these memories, he felt sure he could reproduce them faithfully, and proceeded to approach the tabby sideways, as he had seen Mrs. Grubach's calico do on several occasions.

To his very great surprise, Gregor found that his new nose

once more proved itself a wonder. For he did catch a great wafting smell emanating from the tabby, one which suggested to his mind, without speaking, a kind of comfortably guarded welcome, something like a door into a rich study, left slightly ajar. He wondered what his own glands communicated, but could see no very ready way to control them at this stage in his development. He trotted up to the gentleman cat and pressed his moist pink nose to the slightly darker, grayer nose of his new companion. The smell was very much stronger this close to the source; again he sensed the slightly open door, but now also a kettle of tea boiling just within, and scones with fresh butter laid out ready for a guest, and perhaps a snifter of something already decanted—yet the door still not so open that he could be sure any of that finery was meant for him. What a very great and complex language cats have, Gregor thought, that all this may be transferred without speech, without gesture, but through scent alone!

"That's quite enough," said the tabby. "You are new at this; I will not ask you to embarrass yourself further."

Gregor felt himself at a loss. He understood the other cat well; though he had made little more than a mild meowing, he heard it as a pleasant, deep voice, cultured, slightly foreign—German, perhaps, or Swiss. He was terrified at how his own voice might sound. A kitten, still, his fat making his cheeks puff out and his body very sweetly round instead of the largesse of this grand specimen: Would his greeting sound like a boy's tremulous voice? A castrato or worse? He felt a piercing shame, as often he had when trying to converse with his father on the issues of the day, for no matter what opinion he ventured his father disdained it, even if he himself had defended that same position the evening before, chalking up his son's paucity of intelligence to natural defects in his character and sneering at his efforts to sustain the argument, all the while drinking port Gregor had purchased and sitting upon a couch bought with Gregor's earnings. It was with this burning memory of humiliation fresh in his mind that he spoke:

"Who are you?" He had been too brusque, he saw that immediately. He could smell his own scent now, so strong had his fear of shaming himself become, his mind flooded with the image of a door slammed tight—but creaking open to let a terrified child peer through, trembling with mortification.

"I am the tabby Josef K.," announced the cat calmly, and began to nonchalantly groom his large, slate-colored paw as though Gregor were not standing before him, desperate for approval and comradeship. "And whatever your name may be I can smell that you were a man with a profession just a few days past—I was once a bank clerk, so you see I understand your predicament completely and can even sympathize, though of course it was all so long ago in my case that I can hardly recall the state of having been a bank clerk, which I understand was a common enough profession and for all I know still is, though why anyone would want to spend all day indoors chasing bits of paper money I cannot begin to speculate, I truly cannot. Indeed when I reflect on it—and I have time and disposition and capacity in abundance for such exercises now—I see that catdom is in every way a superior and more marvelous institution than clerkdom. After all, when I chase bits of paper, I really commit to it! Apart from us cats there are all sorts of creatures in the world, wretched, limited, dumb creatures who have no language but mechanical cries without any scent to enrich and deepen them; many of us cats study them and give them names, try to help them, educate them, uplift their moods, and so on. For my part I am quite indifferent to them except when they try to disturb me; I confuse them with one another, for they all look alike, I ignore them when at all possible. But one thing is too obvious to have escaped me, namely, how little inclined they are, compared with us cats, to stick together, how silently and sullenly and with what unspoken hostilities they pass one another by, how only the basest of interests such as food, drink, or breeding can bring them together for a little time in ostensible union—and how often those very interests give rise to violent conflict among them! Consider us cats on the other hand!

One can easily see that we live all together in a heap, all of us, wherever we find ourselves, different as we are from one another on account of numberless profound and infinitesimal modifications that have arisen over the course of time. All in one heap! Of course I am not in a heap now, you might say, but all I had to do was stretch out and you immediately arrived, as if drawn by some invisible force, and though one cannot in seriousness call two cats a heap, they are well on their way! Where there is one there shall be two; where there are two, four cannot be far distant; where there are four, well, might as well give up the game! We are drawn to each other, and nothing can prevent us from satisfying that communal impulse; all our bylaws and institutions, the few we have and that I can be bothered with remembering, are rooted in this longing for the greatest bliss we know, the warm comfort of being together, tail to nose, belly to back, piled one atop the other against the cold of the world! I recall in my life as a man I was hounded from place to place, imprecated with accusations and harangued by men I did not know—what's worse, when I desired a female I could almost never have her; if I wanted drink I would almost certainly have to endure the harsh looks of my landlady; and all day long my vital energy was sapped by folk who had no natural right to it—my employers, my debtors, my parents— everyone, in short, but myself, the one with the most interest in spending it!

I know what you will say, kitten: Do not I have to worry now that some other cat might happen upon me in an alley, bite my ear or sever my tail, have some secret argument with me which I know nothing about, so that I must walk in fear every moment that doom in the form of a Persian or a Siamese might fall on me from the night? Well, certainly, certainly, but this is only the way of the world and one cannot blame the world for continuing in its way. If two cats in black fur appear to escort me away from my provender and to some dank hole where they might assail me more conveniently, well, at least I have a fighting chance to claw their eyes out in turn, where I promise you, in the world of men you will get no such opportunity!"

This entire speech the tabby Josef K delivered by means of a few long, plaintive meows, a bit of purring, and some kneading of his impressive paws against the base of the monument. The rest Gregor understood through his nose and his whiskers, which was, he felt, a most extraordinary thing.

"I am Gregor Samsa," he essayed the technique himself, and found that though he worried about his accent the whole thing was as natural to him as folding a newspaper under his arm and hopping onto the commuter train in the morning had been not so very long ago. "And until Tuesday last I was a traveling salesman, though I could not begin to explain why I should happen to find myself no longer a traveling salesman but, as you see and hear, a very round and furry kitten—or cat, as I seem to be growing at a rapid rate—and as you say nothing about how you came to be the tabby Josef K instead of the bank clerk Josef K, I presume you know nothing about it either, but we are both in the same predicament and in a position to help each other—you to provide introduction for myself into the society of cats, and myself perhaps to provide some understanding of men that you have forgotten, being so long separated from your own transformation." It seemed to him that endless sentences were the natural formulations of the feline tongue, for he did not feel capable of putting an end to any thought at all before he had appended seven or eight more onto the rear of it.

The tabby Josef K stood up and arched his back, stretching first one hind leg and then the other. Two other cats silently arrived and flanked him, their fur cream colored and close fitting with deep brown accents upon their ears and tails and paws. Their pelts were silky and flat, unlike his own unruly coat. They all purred, disconcertingly, in unison. Josef K said:

"Instead, while my comrades Franz and Willem accompany you—say good evening, gentlemen—no, I'm afraid you cannot resist, as I informed you in my earlier statement we cats do long to be together at all times and in all ways, and you are very fortunate that I and my fellows here are so eager and willing to be together in a heap with your own person—you are, you must admit, both a newcomer and a foreigner, and might have it much worse if you understand my meaning, which I think you must. While we all three of us go very efficiently and directly to the Academy for your trial, I will recall an incident from my youth. Did I say your trial? I meant your conviction. Did I say your conviction? I meant your execution. Did I say execution? No, no, good sir, I meant only your introduction to society." The cream-colored cats pressed in on him so closely that Gregor felt himself truly in restraints and was compelled to move along rather quickly with his new comrades as Josef K went on. "Now, I was at the time in one of those inexplicable joyous states of exaltation that everyone must have experienced once or twice as a kitten; I was still quite a kitten myself, having only recently departed the position of bank clerk and entered the position of tabby. Everything delighted me, everything was my concern. I believed that great events were going on around me of which I was the leader and to which I must lend my authoritative voice, things which would quite literally cease to be if I did not run after them and investigate them and wrap my tail around them—and presently something did happen that seemed to justify my wild assumptions. In itself it was nothing very extraordinary, for I have seen many such things often enough since, and more remarkable things, too, but at the time it struck me with all the force of a first impression, one of those impressions that can never be erased and influence a great deal of one's later conduct." And here the two burlier cats physically lifted Gregor between their bodies, hurrying him along down a corridor between buildings and away from the little square near the quay, away from the men carrying the bier and the girl filling her bucket and the fruit seller.

"I encountered, in short, a little company of cats," the tabby Josef K continued, "or rather I did not encounter them but they appeared before me, as cats have their habit of doing. Before that I had been running in darkness a long time, filled with a premonition of great things—of mice and of the possibility of not-too-rotten fish to be discovered but also of gripping a certain blue by the neck and mounting her, as well as settling a score with a couple of fellows who had been rude to me and squashed my ear, leaping upon them until they accepted my domination completely. I had run in darkness for a long time, just as we are doing now, up and down, listening sharply to everything, led on by vague, unfocused desires for everything I have already mentioned, and then I suddenly came to a stop with the feeling that I was in the right place, and looking up I saw suddenly that it was a bright day, only a little hazy, and everywhere was a riot of intoxicating smells; I greeted the morning with an uncertain growling in my throat, when—as if I had conjured them up out of some well of darkness, to the accompaniment of terrible sounds such as I had never heard before even when I was a man, seven cats stepped into the light. Had I not clearly seen that they were cats and that they themselves brought those sounds with them—though I could not understand how they were producing it—I would have run away at once, but things were more or less as I have stated, so I stayed. At that time I still knew almost nothing of that peculiar creative gift for music with which the feline race is uniquely endowed—certainly you have some inkling of it already having heard my humble symphonies—though music had surrounded me as a perfectly natural and indispensable element of existence while I was a man, I had not yet discovered it as a cat, and so all the more astonishing to me were these seven great musicians, standing before me, not speaking, not singing, but remaining generally quite silent, intently silent, as though silent with a purpose—but from the empty air they conjured music. Everything was music, the lifting and settling down of their feet, certain turns of their heads, their running and their abruptly standing still, the positions they took up in relation to one another, the symmetrical patterns they produced by one cat kneading the belly of another with his front paws and the rest doing likewise until the first bore all the weight of the other six, or by all lying flat on the ground and whirling their tails in several complicated revolutions, and none made a false move or note, not even the last cat, though he was a little unsure compared to the others, did not always seem to enjoy being the one whose belly was kneaded rather than a kneader, who sometimes hesitated on the stroke of the downbeat, but yet was uncertain and lesser only by comparison with the superb performance of the others, and even if he had been much more uncertain, which is to say quite uncertain, indeed, he could not have done very much harm, the others, great maestros all of them, having kept the rhythm so precisely. But it is too much to say that I saw them, that I actually saw them at all. They appeared from somewhere; I greeted them as fellow cats. And although I was profoundly confused by the sounds that accompanied them, they were cats nevertheless—cats like you and me, and you may perceive being at least somewhat intelligent that I have a secondary narrative purpose in saying so. But I regarded them by force of habit simply as cats I happened to meet upon my way, and felt a profound wish to approach them and exchange scents and bristlings; they were quite near to me as well, cats certainly much older than I, and sleek, rather than of the woolly-haired breed shared by myself and yourself, yet not at all alien in size or shape, and indeed quite familiar to me, for I had seen many such or similar cats throughout Prague. But while I was still involved in these reflections—and reflections do involve me deeply, one might say I can hardly be shaken out of them no matter how much a soul might wish to interrupt and silence me—no, he will not do it, or I will scratch him soundly, or have my fellows do it if I do not wish to dull my claws by the action!—the music gradually became deafening, literally knocking the breath out of me and pushing me by brute melodic force far from those little cats, quite against my will—why, just as you have been swept!—and while I howled as if some noxious pain were being inflicted upon me, my mind could attend to nothing but that music that seemed to come from everywhere at once, from the heights, from the depths, from everywhere, surrounding any-one who might listen—how can humans hear nothing of this?—overwhelming his senses, crushing him, and over his in-sensate body still blowing its quiet horns. And then a respite came, for I was too spent, too enervated, too beggared by their voices to endure any more, a respite came and I beheld again the seven cats carrying out their revolutions, making their cir-cus leaps. I longed to call out to them despite their aloof natures, to beg them to enlighten me, poor kitten who still felt as a man of position feels that he could ask anyone anything and receive a sensible answer. But hardly had I begun my interrogation, hardly did I feel as if I was getting toward good and familiar cattish terms with the seven of them, when their psychic music began again, stole my wits away, whirled me in circles as if I were one of the musicians and not merely a victim of their strange spell, cast me here and there, no matter how I begged for mercy. The sounds rescued me finally from their own violence by driving me into a labyrinth of wooden boxes that rose around that alley, though I had never noticed them before, when my business as a man took me briskly from place to place—but then it trapped me wholly, kept my belly pressed to the earth, though that vibratory music still echoed in the space behind me, egging me on like a dog chasing me down. Briefly I thought I had escaped it, and I snatched a moment to get my breath back. I must admit that I was less surprised by the artistry of the seven cats—it was incomprehensible to me, and also quite definitely beyond my capabilities—at least then—than by their courage in facing so openly the music of their own souls—for surely that's what it was, their power to endure it so calmly without turning away from its cacophony, its strength. But now from my hiding hole I saw more closely that it was not so much coolness or disinterest as the most exquisite tension that fueled their performance; those limbs, so apparently sure in their movements quivered at every step with a perpetual apprehensive stiffness; as if rigid with despair the cats kept their eyes fixated on one another, and their tails, whenever the tension weakened for a moment, drooped miserably. It could not be fear of failure that agitated them so deeply; cats do not worry themselves over failure as men do, for a cat cannot fail—if a

THE TWO CATS TOSSED GREGOR INTO A DANK CORNER OF THE ROOM.

creature fails, he is not a cat, and if he is a cat, he cannot fail. But then why were they so afraid?"

Gregor felt that he knew. Had he not held himself in such a tension for days now, unsure of his new body, feeling as though he held himself in this world only by force of will, terrified that it had always been so, that he had always known it was so, and for a moment, just a moment, while he slept, he had let that will slip and all these horrors had resulted? But he felt that, when flanked by two brown-eared creatures with no apparent purpose but to be large and threatening in his direction, it was not the time to interrupt another fellow's story. And, indeed, the tabby Josef K wrinkled his silky muzzle in such a way that he recalled a professor expectantly awaiting answers from a recalcitrant classroom.

"Well, what do you think happened? I called out to them, my best meow, but they—incredible, incredible—made no reply. Cats who make no answer to another cat are guilty of a great offense. A hiss or a growl, surely, these I could have accepted, but nothing at all? Perhaps they were not cats at all. Could I not hear on close examination the subdued cries with which they encouraged one another, drew one another's attention to rising difficulties or coming periods of rest, warned one another against mistakes. Could I not see the last and youngest, to which most of the cries were addressed, the little mackerel not unlike you in his chubby accoutrement, his stripes like a small tiger's, stealing tiny glances at me as though he dearly wished to reply but refrained, for his fellows would not have allowed it? But why should they not allow it, the very thing that our laws unconditionally demand? I became so indignant at the thought and at once the music lost its power over me. Those cats were breaking the law. Great magicians though they might have been, but the law was valid for them, too! I knew the laws quite well, though I was still a kitten. And having recognized them as criminals I noticed another thing. They had good reason for remaining silent, if they had any good sense of shame. For how were they conducting themselves? Because of all the music I had not noticed it before, but they had flung away all shame, the wretched toms were doing the very thing that is most natural to man but most ridiculous and indecent to a cat—they were walking on their hind legs! Fie on them! They were showing their nakedness, blatantly displaying it, they were doing it as though it were an admirable thing. And when, even for a moment, they yielded to their more proper instincts and their paws happened to all rest upon the ground, they were appalled, as if their very nature was a mortal error, hastily snatching up their paws again, their eyes begging forgiveness for having slid into animalism. Another cat might have asked, Has the world turned on its head? But not I. That was the beginning of understanding for Josef K, who apprehended with all his powers that these cats had been, not very long ago indeed, men, as Josef K had been!" The tabby let loose a long, ragged meow of emphasis and also by means of ending his story.

The two large, silky cats pressed in on Gregor, crushing his soft feline ribs. Suddenly he felt that his roundness, so pleasing to his sister, might be the death of him. He inquired whether there was more to the story, to the strange music, whether he, Gregor, was meant to take some moral lesson from the tale, some edification with which to enrich his own experience as a cat.

"That is all there is and there is no more. You will find that, in life as in literature, most episodes are arbitrary, confusing, and not meant for your benefit. I took you for an educated tom, sir, in which case you would have read your German classics and be quite accustomed to a narrator who only loves to hear himself speak—you must admit I speak very well, with many masculine and robust subclauses, romantic dashes, and surprising punctuation—and forgets what the purpose of telling the story was in the first place something like two-thirds of the way through. This is considered traditional! I believe I have shown myself to be quite a high class of cat. There was much symbolism in my monologue if you cared to listen—the music of the seven cats stood at once for the peculiar way in which you must have noticed we felines speak—those seven cats were telling me their life stories all at once, all their woes, their bank clerk sorrows, and the terror of waking up a cat; it's not really very interesting except as a symbol for how I, Josef K, am cleverer than most other cats, whether they used to be men or not, and as a warning that your smallest prancing step, the way you lift your adorable paws and wriggle your sweet little pink nose when you are afraid, reveals to me your entire life story, everything you could ever wish to keep secret and you cannot help revealing these things to me, so truly you are entirely helpless in my power, and during your trial you will not be allowed to lie in any fashion, nor will you be able to, for I will see through it. In addition, the whole chapter was an allegory for the Bohemian anarchist movement and the essential unknowability of the world. Didn't you notice?"

Gregor admitted he had not. He felt deep shame.

"I used a great number of techniques," sniffed Josef K with reproach.

"But how can there be a trial? Am I under arrest? And why is it all proceeding so strangely? I haven't done anything."

"Now you're starting again," said the larger of the two burly cats, Franz, dipping into a low alleyway and dragging him along with the brute force of his furry shoulder. "We don't answer questions like that." They all crept on their bellies over and under several unpleasant things, greasy pipes and broken masonry and overturned rubbish canisters. Finally they squeezed in single file through an opening in a crumbling, moldering wall and into a large area crawling with cats of every description and color, piled together in decadent heaps just as Josef K had described, some of their paws trailing in huge saucers of milk, some of them slurping kippers with relish and miowling at one another drunkenly. It reminded Gregor on the whole of gentlemen's clubs of which he had never been a member, not because he could not afford it—rather he was very near to being able to purchase membership, and at that point the clubs habitually allowed you to attend on a trial basis—but because he was not well liked by the other gentlemen of his economic station. He was short and dark and a salesman besides, which seemed to them an unsavory occupation. And besides he had neither wife nor child nor particularly distinguished family name, and what could he bring to such a club, what could he add that they did not already have? He considered that all of this had been communicated to him by the angles of the board members' eyebrows and the tenor of their very polite promises to take his future membership under advisement rather than by direct address, and perhaps the ways in which men and cats were different were perhaps very small, indeed.

Just at that moment the two beefy cats snatched Gregor by the scruff, their teeth biting into him painfully, and tossed him without too much trouble—for he was still a kitten, albeit a large one, soft and pliable and fluffy—into a dank corner of the room and then stood in front of him like two dark walls, creating a little cell out of which he had little hope of forcing his way. Gregor cried out in alarm and fright, scrabbling his large white paws under his captors' heavy bellies, an act they seemed to notice not at all.

Willem, who could be differentiated from Franz by a blaze of dark brown on his chest and a certain blunt fatness to his face, yawned so widely that his face seemed to split open from ear to ear.

"The way you're carrying on, it's worse than a child. Your little paws wiggling say there has been a mistake and you're such a good kitty, a sweet kitty, not a bad, naughty, guilty one at all. Well, what is it you want? Do you want to get this great, bloody trial of yours over with quickly? We're just cats, that's all we are. Muscle. Junior officers like us hardly know one end of Prague from the other: all we've got to do is do what K. says and get paid for it in kippers and sparrows. That's all we are; that's all we care about. Josef K said, 'Come on, there's a new one, best round him up before he makes trouble,' and we reported to the docks just in time. Mind you, if you have a few scraps of trout or whatnot hidden away somewhere, what we can do is make sure that our testimony says this here is a right sort of fellow, not a lick of trouble. There's no mistake there. We can make it easy on you. Our authorities as far as I know, and I only know the lowest grades, don't go out looking for guilt among the public; it's the guilt that draws them out, like it says in the law, and they have to send us out. That's the law. Where d'you think there'd be any mistake there?"

"I don't know this law you mean," said Gregor. "I haven't done anything at all, and if it's an issue of my having been a traveling salesman a few days ago, why, Josef K was also a man, and a bank clerk besides, which is a wretched sort of profession, and so it can't be that my crime is simply one of birth."

"As to that, I was born an insurance man," Willem purred. "I had two sons and they were both only so-so in the face, but what else can you ask, with an old tom like me as a father? I was going about life as fine as you please, not rich but not poor, not fat but not hungry, and when bad things happened to other people I felt happy about it, because it meant that I had work. You shouldn't judge me for that, but given the circumstances I'll be generous and say you can if you like, if it makes you feel better, more comforted in your hour of need. But then, one morning, I woke up and I was just a ball of cuddly soft kitten, and nothing anyone did could set me to rights! Well, my boys were only so-so in the soul as well, it turned out, and they pulled my ears and shaved my tail and tried to set my whiskers on fire, so I took flight out a window, and there you have the story of Willem, who is now a bachelor, thank you very much, and a respectable policecat with as much mackerel as he can chew, most days. The life of a police officer is a good one, I must say—one is safe from most predations and one gets to pounce on a great number of unsuspecting folk."

"Do you never worry that you pounce upon the innocent?" pleaded Samsa.

"It doesn't trouble me. If they were innocent, they wouldn't have gotten arrested. After all, I've never been arrested."

Franz, whose face was a good deal narrower, as in the habit of some Ægyptian statues, turned his head while keeping his body firmly in place, imprisoning poor Samsa.

"If you're curious, I was a psychiatrist with my own sanatorium—lovely place, very clean, as humane as such can be, given that they are built to house the inhumane. But I had a comfortable office, and a very fine rug, several kinds of brandy, and a mistress in another city, which is the best place for mistresses. I did not wish to marry, for it did not interest me, and children interested me far less than the latest journals on abnormal behavior. I felt reasonably optimistic about the course of my life and hoped to make a discovery or two before I died and to be bothered as little as possible, which, truly, is not very likely in a sanatorium, but that is what God gave us morphine for, is it not, Willem? And yet, like my fellow officer here, I went to bed one night and suffered unpleasant dreams such as I often had when ingesting a great deal of dairy and woke in my current state, though somewhat smaller, with what I may humbly suggest were the finest set of paws ever set on a cat. Unfortunately the fate of cats in Bohemian sanatoriums is more often some poor schizophrenic's supper or a psychotic's personal toy, and I immediately realized my danger and made use of the front exit. Be grateful, I say. I once knew a man who woke up a cockroach."

Gregor was not depressed by these tales of unfortunate transformations but rather energized. He suggested that they might, if they put their intellects to the task, discover the ultimate metaphysical reason behind their situations and uncover some method of reversing them and returning to their old lives. But his eager imprecations were greeted with laughter.

"If you're unhappy with your affairs, so much the worse for you, then," said Willem. "Life has worked out all to my satisfaction."

Franz concurred. "As we are not on trial, we have no particular worries."

"It probably exists only in our heads," Gregor said without much hope. He wanted, in some way, to insinuate himself into the thoughts of the cats, to reshape those thoughts to his benefit or to make himself at home there. But Willem just said dismissively, "What do you want reasons for? You broke the law, you go to trial, you take your punishment. Metaphysics doesn't figure into it. Not our field."

"But I haven't done anything!"

Franz joined in and said, "Look at this, Willem, he doesn't even know feline law and at the same time insists he's innocent. As for it being all in our heads, I think I would have noticed if I had gone mad. It was my profession, after all."

"You're quite right, but we can't get him to understand a thing," said the other cat.

Gregor stopped talking with them. "Do I," he thought to himself, "do I really have to carry on getting tangled up with the chattering of lackeys like this? They admit that they are of the lowest position. They're talking about things of which they don't have the slightest understanding, anyway. It's only because of their stupidity that they're able to be so sure of themselves. I just need a few words with Josef K and everything will be in-comparably clearer, much clearer than a long conversation with these two can make it."

He walked up and down the free space in his little cell a couple of times. He had to put an end to this display.

"Take me to your superior, the tabby Josef K," he said.

"As soon as he wants to see you. Not before," said the one called Willem. "And now my advice to you," he added, "is to sit down, stay calm, and wait and see what's to be done with you. If you take our advice, you won't tire yourself out thinking about philosophical things to no purpose. You need to pull yourself together, for there's a lot of sitting and listening to your personal faults that's going to be required of you. You've behaved toward us decently enough so far, but you forget that we, whatever we are, we're still free cats and you're not, and that's quite an advantage and an indication you ought to take seriously that we are in all the important ways superior to you."

Gregor stood still for some time. Perhaps, if he barged into them head-first, the two of them would not be able to stand in his way—perhaps that would be the simplest way to settle the whole thing, by bringing it to a head, as it were. But maybe they would grab him, and if he were thrown down on the ground he would lose all the advantage he, in a certain respect, had over them, having been a man much more recently. But perhaps it was no advantage at all, since he had no notion of how to compete in a feline brawl, or any brawl, for that matter, as that sort of thing was rarely required of salesmen. So he decided on the more certain solution, the way things would go in the natural course of events, and curled up with his tail brought round to hide his face, without another word either from him or from the burly cats.

He pawed helplessly and a little pathetically at the stone

floor and thought back fondly on the half-frozen tossed-out fish he had enjoyed earlier. For just a moment, then, between the window of his old apartment and the square where he had met Josef K, he had felt well and confident—now all that good feeling was gone. At the same time, though, he asked himself, this time looking at it from his own point of view, what reason he could have to go on at all. It would have been so pointless to kill himself when he had been a man and unhappy, so that even if he had wanted to, the pointlessness would have made him unable. And now he was a cat with no clear idea how such a thing could be accomplished, without the advantages of hanging, poisoning, or a respectable revolver. All those methods were unavailable and seemed to intend on remaining so. If only he could have a bit of schnapps, he could clear his head, but of course that was impossible, and he could no more discern what a cat would quaff in place of schnapps than how a cat might manage suicide.

Then he was so startled by a shout to him from the wider room that he struck his sharp teeth against his tongue.

"The tabby Josef K is going to speak!" the voice said, and it was Franz's voice. It was only the shout that startled him, this curt, abrupt, military shout, that he would not have expected from a cat called Franz, nor any of his friends.

Gregor managed to get a good look by settling back on

his haunches, the very act Josef K had called ridiculous and indecent in a cat, so that his head rose up over the haunches of
his captors. The tabby was preening at the front of the crowd, a
little mouse corpse pinned to his furry breast, bleeding freely,
looking from this distance very much like a gay red carnation.

"Honored members of the Academy of Cats!" he began,
and the room fell into reverent silence, awaiting his speech,
which Samsa felt would be as long-winded as his previous one
and all the worse for it being aimed at his own person instead
of some rambling reminiscence.

"You have done me the honor of allowing my testimony
to be entered in the case of the brown and white mackerel Gregor S, on account of my former life as an ape. I regret that my
testimony will not be perfect and complete, since it is now
nearly five years since I was an ape, a short time, perhaps, according to the calendar, but an infinitely long time to scamper
through at full speed, as I have done, more or less accompanied
by excellent mentors, good advice, applause and orchestral
music, and yet essentially I have been a cat who walked by himself, noble, self-sufficient, all places alike to me. I could never
have achieved what I have done had I been stubbornly set on
clinging to my origins, to the memories of my former life. In
fact, to give up being human was the chief achievement I set for
myself; free cat that I became, I refused to submit to the yokes

that bound me as a man. As if in revenge, however, my memory of that life has closed the door against me more and more
as the years go by. I have the feeling that at some point in the
whole affair I might have returned to my life as it was, through
an archway as wide as heaven and as small as a pinprick, returned through whatever means I arrived, to discover one
morning, waking up from anxious dreams, that I had been
changed into a respectable man. But as I spurred myself on
through the society of cats, in my chosen career as a tom among
toms, that opening, if ever it existed, twisted slowly shut behind
me, narrowed and shrank to nothing. I felt more comfortable in
the world of cats and it suited me better; the strong wind that
blew after me out of my past, the strong wind full of a bank
clerk's concerns, a husband's anxieties, a father's angers, began to
slacken; today it is only a gentle puff of air that plays about my
paws as I run with my brothers and sisters through the dirty,
beautiful streets of Prague, and the opening through which it
blows, that leads back to my former life, through which I, the
tabby Josef K, once came, has grown so small that even if I
wished to get back to it, I should have to scrape the skin from
my belly to crawl through. To put it plainly—and you know
how I dislike to put things plainly!—life as an ape, gentlecats,
insofar as something of that kind lies behind one, lies as far behind *him*," and Gregor understood quite sharply that it was he

who was meant, "as it does behind me. Yet still he feels a tickle—all of us did, the small kitten and the great old queen alike."

It caused Gregor Samsa a very great pain in his stomach to hear the tabby refer to a passage back to that life he had had before. He wished nothing so much as to wake up and find it all some horrible phantasm caused by too much dairy, and to hear Josef K idly ruminate on his feeling that it might be done if only he wished it enough caused his heart to bend inward in a bout of bitterness. All the cats seemed to be looking at him with suspicion and reproach—but then, cats looked at everything that way, did they not?

"What I have to present of the citizen Gregor S will contribute little new to the Academy; we can see he was a man, he does not argue the point, I assure you. In fact, he was the worst of all men—a salesman who let his family trample his soul underfoot and never once told them to step lightly, who had no personal pride, which we cats know is paramount in a creature of any sort of worth whatsoever, whose entire ambition was to remain unbothered by his father and to perhaps pay for a few violin lessons for his sister. All this, fellow Academy members, I have observed in his gait, the angle of his tail, the quivering of his whiskers in the night wind. The kitten Gregor S could not lie to me if he tried to, and he did not try—he is not clever enough to try! Even I in my most debased state, I was not so utterly dominated as he—for a memory floats up to me now of having been most cruelly reprimanded by my employer at the bank over some small slight, some mix-up of paperwork that in the larger scheme could not have mattered less but caused my employer to get very red in the face, to yell until he was sweating profusely, and myself to shrink and cower in his presence, for I had then not the soul of a cat and knew no better than to crawl on my belly when another man challenged me. I should have raked a paw across his face and had his ear for breakfast! But men are shallow, mouselike creatures at heart, scurrying in terror here and there rather than standing up and using their teeth for Nature's intended purpose. The kitten Gregor S had no way out of his life, and yet so entirely prostrate had he become that he did not even seek a way out, nor would he have understood what was meant by the phrase. Now, I fear that you may not understand what I mean by 'way out.' I use the expression in its fullest and most popular sense. I deliberately do not say that he had no, nor did he seek, 'freedom.' As a cat, we all know this thing, and know that men have no proper notion of it. In fact, may I say that all too often men are betrayed by the word *freedom*, which is often bleated by trumpets in their arenas but to which their world provides no road. Cats know freedom; we eat it and drink it, we know it wholly, as a mother or lover. What do men know? And as their poor reflective mockery of 'freedom' is counted among the most sublime feelings in their warped philosophies, so the corresponding disillusionment is a kind of hell. I recall as a man in a suit and tails—how amusing was it that even then my wardrobe showed my true nature!—attending variety theaters in which a couple of acrobats performed on trapezes situated high in the roof. They swung in long curves, they rocked to and fro, they leapt high into the air, they floated down into each other's arms, one hanging by the hair from the teeth of the other. Then I was moved in my bones and thought it beautiful. Now I say: 'That is human freedom.' Controlled movement, bound up in ropes and knots, bound to other humans by clenched jaw and torn hair. Now we know what freedom truly is—if there is a knotted rope to be had, then we chase it with gusto and shred it in our claws! Or not! As we like it!

"People often praise the universal progress made by the cat community throughout the ages, and probably mean by that more particularly the progress in our communal knowledge and wisdom. Certainly our knowledge of ourselves and the world is progressing, its advance is irresistible, it progresses at ever-accelerating speeds, always faster than men's, certainly faster than mice, birds, or fish, and no one here may seriously argue that dogs outstrip us at any contest of wits. But what is there to praise in this? We are cats; naturally we become more clever. It is like praising someone because with the years he manages to grow older and, in consequence, comes nearer and nearer to death. Moreover, that is a natural yet ugly process, whereas the progress we see among ourselves is hard won and sublime. In the world of men I see only decline, but in ours I see something more awesome, more complex.

"I do not mean that earlier generations of cats were essentially worse than ours, only younger, and that was their great advantage—it was easier then to get them to speak and mingle in a jocular way, for fewer of them had ever been bank clerks or had any human ancestry to feel ashamed about. Indeed, it is the sense of wholly cattish life and the possibilities of that life that thrill us so deeply when we listen to those old and strangely simple stories told by the dowager-queens and grandfather-toms here tonight. Here and there in their speech we catch a curiously significant phrase that seems to prefigure the New Cat, and we would almost like to leap to our feet, to cry out—yes, there, I see myself in what you say! Yet we are silent. I cannot put it another way—previous generations had not quite yet gotten so catlike as we are today, catdom was still a loose confederation, where now it is beginning to be a great nation. I know there are toms here who were in the war—oh, which war it hardly matters, but some of you were soldiers and brave men, some of you faced death and instead became cats. And while I am sure at the time you were alarmed and not a little put out by the whole business, I say to you there was a logic in your change of clothes, for in the ancient world cats were given their due and worshipped as creatures standing between life and death, guardians of the threshold, and in our paws we weighed the human soul against a feather, and both were toys for our enjoyment. Our generation is lost—we stand between men and cats, more wonderful than either, yet less pure and more miserable, for we carry our unhappiness with us, and we were all miserable bastards before we grew tails, were we not? What has happened to the world where such transformations can now be expected to occur?

"I can understand our hesitation to open those old questions—it is not hesitation but the thousandth forgetting of a dream dreamt a thousand times and forgotten a thousand times, and who can damn us for merely forgetting for the thousandth time what giants we had hoped to be as men? What world we had hoped to make with out meaty, five-fingered, devil-bethumbed paws? Some of us discovered that to be ripped from those ambitions and deposited in a furry body was no tragedy—some thought not, and they are not allowed to supper with us fashionable felines. When our first fathers turned from men to animals they doubtless had no notion that their aberration was to be an endless one; they could still see, literally, the crossroads where something could have been taken back, made other than it was. It seemed an easy task to turn back whenever they pleased, and if they did not immediately ring Parliament and demand that a health committee be convened on their behalf and an epidemic declared, it was merely because they fancied it would be pleasant to enjoy a cat's life for a little while longer; it was not yet a genuine cat's life, though it had become already intoxicatingly beautiful to them, and so they strayed farther into the streets and discovered the pleasures of hunting and breeding queens and kipper-heads tossed out with as little care as a girl plucking petals. They did not yet know what we can guess at, contemplating the course of all our histories: that change begins in the soul before it appears in ordinary existence, and that, when they began to enjoy a cat's life, they must already have begun to possess cats' souls and were by no means so near their starting point as they had once thought, or as their eyes feasting on all kittenish joys might try to persuade them.

"But what has all this to do with Gregor S? I do not try to be mysterious. I see you nodding—you know what I know. What testimony do we need to know: he is a miserable bastard and has no more good instinct than a hound raced half to death. Change begins in the soul, and he must have had a cat's soul somewhere, a cat's soul that was being crushed by the attentions of his ungrateful, brutish family who wish to catch him up in their arms even when he did not wish to be cuddled or coddled at all and squeeze him to death for their own pleasure. And yet he bore it, he bore it all, without a scratch or a hiss or the smallest standing up for his pride, and with as little joy or affect as he shows us now, even though he has a fine coat and a shapely tail and, given time, could have any queen here; he owns no liveliness or vigor. He did violence to his feline self in that apartment, and violence to his soul now—can nothing rouse this man? He shows his throat when no one's growled at him to do it! I am his prosecutor. In one paw I weigh him and in the other, well, I dare not show the counterweight. He stands accused—"

And Gregor felt great alarm, for he sensed the ending of the proceedings when they had not rightly even begun.

"Of what? Of what am I accused?" he cried piteously.

"He stands accused," the tabby Josef K went on unperturbed as if he had not spoken. "How do you find him, my fellow Academy members?"

"GUILTY," came the answering howl, and then all went silent.

# IV.

Someone must have been telling lies about Gregor Samsa; he knew he had done nothing wrong.

He purred miserably to himself and gnawed briefly at a scrap of mouse that had been brought for him. "It has all gone so horribly wrong." He addressed himself only to Franz's ample, silky backside, which was turned firmly toward him as a kind of jail door. Other cats milled about somewhere beyond his well-padded rump, enervated after the excitement of the trial. "I'm not trying to be a grand orator and arouse your pity; that's probably more than I'm capable of anyway. I'm sure my defense can speak far better than I can; it is part of the job of a defense in general to do so. And I'm sure I shall have a defense, even though the verdict has already been read. It's not a trial without a defense. The prosecution came before the accusation, after all. Perhaps this is merely how cats understand the law? All that I want is a public discussion of a public wrong. Listen: Ten days ago I was changed utterly—this whole trial itself is something I laugh about when you put it beside the essential point of my being a cat, but that's no matter. You came for me when I had no way of preparing myself. Maybe it was all a mistake! Maybe the order had been given to arrest some house painter who had been transformed into—what did you say of your unfortunate friend?—a cockroach, yes, that seems possible after what has been said, someone who is as innocent as I am but had a worse time of it in the luck of the animal draw, as it were. Or perhaps he had a cockroach's soul, as Josef K has opined! However it sorted out for that poor, benighted wretch, you came for me, you and Willem, two police thugs. You could not have treated me more roughly if I had been a violent robber. Josef K talked at me till I was sick of it. And even that was not enough, I had to sit through his prosecutorial arguments, which were endless and went nowhere, I must say. Ægypt! Can you imagine. It was not easy to stay calm, but I managed to do so and was completely calm when I asked all of you why it was that I was under arrest. What do you think any of you louts answered? Nothing at all, that's what. Perhaps you really did know nothing—you just made your arrest and were satisfied. But I cannot believe you are wholly without gentle inclinations, that you view me entirely with contempt and have no pity in you whatever, Franz. I cannot believe that. But I repeat: This whole affair has caused me nothing but unpleasantness and irritation. But could it not also have had some far worse consequences? After all, what comes after arrest, trial, and conviction—even if their order is entirely chaotic and unhinged—but execution?"

Franz looked mildly over his shoulder, his long white whiskers showing against gleaming fur. "You are concerned that you will be executed?"

"Like a dog," Gregor confirmed.

"Everything seems so simple to you, doesn't it," Franz yawned, his yellow eyes bulging, "so you think we should bring the matter to a peaceful close, do you. Claw out your throat or drown you in the river? No, no, that won't do. Mind you, on the other hand I certainly wouldn't want you to think there's hope for you. No, why should you think that? You're simply under arrest, nothing more than that. That's what I had to do, arrest you, that's what I've done and now I've seen how you've taken it."

"How else should I have taken it? Please, please do tell me how I might have behaved that would have altered the events of this evening in the smallest fashion. And where has Willem

SOMEONE MUST HAVE BEEN TELLING LIES ABOUT GREGOR SAMSA.

gone? Do you think you can contain me yourself? I could run off at any moment! I'm quite good on these paws, I tell you."

"Willem has affairs. We all do; we can't spend all day trying former salesmen. He'll return presently, if he has a mind to. Willem can be somewhat distracted by parades, queens in heat, rats, passing bits of dust, he really is a bit of a fool. And you will not run off."

"How do you know I won't?"

"You never ran off from your father, and he was far worse to you than we are. After all, we address you courteously most of the time and provide for your supper, we try to teach you things, and in the morning we will all go off to our hunting or our preening or our napping in sunbeams, and any one of those is more than your fat patriarch occupies himself with in a week."

Gregor sunk his handsome face in his fuzzy chest. A bit of fish clung there in his ruff and he made haste to deal with it, scrupulously licking his coat, though bits of fur kept getting caught in his mouth in a most undignified way. He began to wonder if he really understood at all what was meant by "arrest" or "trial" or any of this business. It seemed to be formulated by a particularly clever devil for the purposes of torment alone, but he could see no purpose behind it, no reason at all. In his former life, if he were to—God forbid it—be arrested, he expected he would know what crime he had committed and be somewhat ashamed already when the police arrived, chagrined at least a little, perhaps somewhat relieved to be finally caught out, and he would go to the docket and have a fine attorney, for he had some money, had he not? The attorney would cross-examine and perhaps get him off with a light sentence and send him home in time to see his sister graduate from the conservatory he still dreamed of sending her to, and he would be a criminal, yes, but still understand his place in the world. Yet he could not be entirely certain this is how it would go, could he? The soul of a cat in the body of a man—what lawyer, what judge, did that not describe, sitting behind a bench in a white wig, licking his paws and waiting for the pounce, or else prowling the night streets seeking out easy prey: innocent, fat creatures who would go into the gallows without much of a fight, their paws padding everywhere, silent, unseen, shadows appearing and disappearing as they liked. "The world is full of beasts who are men and men who are beasts," thought Gregor. "I suppose my little incident is symbolic, like Josef K's dancing cats. Nothing else. Symbolism is depressing; its meaning is always deferred. Nothing is what it is, only what it means, and I mean nothing but that the world is ugly and men are uglier still." What, Gregor wondered, did he dream that night, when he tossed and turned and grew long tufted ears and a tail like a quill pen and such long teeth, what did he dream that was so full of a cat's de-sires, a cat's thoughts, a cat's motions and morals? For surely, in the end, it was the dreams that did it, for dreams are symbols; even Gregor, who had busied his life with the eating of pota-toes and accumulating of compound interest, knew that, and knowing that he knew he must have dreamt something signif-icant in order to enter into this world where meaning was for-ever further off than he could reach. Men before the gallows are always philosophical, and now he supposed that cats were, too.

"What did *you* dream, the night before you changed into an animal?" he asked his jailor, so that he could cease asking himself.

"The tabby Josef K does not like us to remember our lives, for that opening he speaks of is always behind us, the cloaca of the soul, and he fears to fall into it, much as he pretends it is not so; but I will tell you what I dreamt of, for I suspect that you dreamt it, too, your night of anxious dreams. I suspect we all dreamt it, and perhaps one day before death we will dream it again, or its reverse, its mirror, everything happening in oppo-sition to the original so that when we leave our corpses on the street they are suddenly once more old Bohemian men gone to paunch and wrinkles, with tattered waistcoats half a century old barely covering their nakedness. I dreamed of an insect—I could not tell what sort, only that it was blackish brown and

large, though its size changed often and sometimes it could hide
from me, scurrying beneath furniture, and sometimes it was so
large it filled my vision, a terrible six-legged thing that squeaked
wretchedly and waggled its miserable wings as if it meant to fly
away from itself. I dreamed this insect dwelled in an apartment
little different from the one I recall from my days as a man, with
chairs and sofas and sinks indistinguishable from my own, but
not my own, only of the same type and general appearance, for
there is little difference in the homes of men of our station, so
eager are we to belong and style ourselves alike so as to avoid
the slightest glimpse of strangeness leaking into our waistcoats
and sinks and evening chairs. The insect rose up before me as if
to injure me, but in the end it did not, merely slumped down
and crawled into a bed that was not my bed but looked very
much like it, burrowing its triangular head under the covers
and weeping softly. As I watched, the insect tossed its rigid
body as if occupied by anxious dreams of its own, and I must
have let my head droop and sleep in the night, for when I woke,
and it woke, the insect had become a novelist with pomade in
his hair, lying on his back and staring at the ceiling as if he had
no notion of how he had changed or that he had. He lay on his
soft, sweaty back and saw, as he lifted his head a little, his flat abdomen covered in a striped shirtfront. The blanket, just about
ready to slide off completely, stayed in its proper place. His

legs—so few now—pitifully thin compared to the rest of his more or less healthy person, lay motionless on the mattress.

"'What's happened to me?' he said softly, and I had no answer for him. I only dreamed; I could not help. His room, a proper room for a human being if somewhat too small, lay quietly between the four well-known walls. The novelist's glance then turned to the window. The dreary weather—the raindrops were falling audibly onto the metal window ledge—made him quite melancholy. 'If I keep sleeping for a while, all this will disappear,' he whispered, putting his hands over his face. 'O God, what a relentless job I've chosen! Day in, day out, the pen in my hand alone. The stresses of writing are much greater than I ever imagined, and, in addition to that, I have to cope with the problems of meaning, the worries about metaphor and symbols, irregular bad food, fleeting human relationships that never come from the heart, friends who look at me and see only an investor or a poor sack of a man with the soul of a crawling thing. To hell with it all! None of it has a meaning—well, today I meant to give it one; I meant to take up each of my stories and give them new endings, in which all would be explained and made well, in which no one could be left wondering how they had managed to get themselves into any unhappy state, in which the world would be well ordered and calm. I meant to do all of this, but now I find myself this morning changed utterly into a beast, and all I know is fear, my heart degraded and alone, my lungs filling up with water that might as well be tears.' I tried to argue with the novelist, to tell him that, on the contrary, he had been a monster that made my soul shiver with cold, but now he seemed quite respectable, if in need of a bath and a solid breakfast; but he would not hear it, only went to his desk and held sheaf after sheaf of paper to his heart, tearing them into pieces. He coughed horribly, quite horribly, and a spot of blood spattered upon the wall. 'I cannot speak so that I am understood,' he whispered. 'I try to speak like a man, well and orderly, and all that comes out is a series of alien clicks and squeaks full of dark patterns and crawling, anxious terrors, and I am never understood and my stories are warrens where no one may find their way. I know myself, and I know I am a monster, that I have always been a monster—it was only that, for a brief moment, no one knew it, and I looked somewhat like a man, from the right angle—but I am a creature and a monster and I know it, I have always known it.' He slid back again into his earlier position. 'This getting up early,' he moaned, 'makes a man quite melancholy.' And at that moment, I believe, I became a cat, not in the dream but in the world—in the dream I remained a man, and though never before had I felt so uncharitably toward a soul, I suddenly found the novelist tiresome and wished only to be about my own business and cease listening to his desolate speech; besides, the sun was streaming in the window in a most enticing manner, and I thought I spied a bit of string in the corner, and both of these seemed infinitely more absorbing than the novelist, who in the end was more endearing as an insect. This is the essence of a cat's psychology: we can only endure humans for so long before, well, there is a sunbeam or a bit of fish in the larder, and who can really be asked to listen to modernist symbolism when such things are at hand? I curled up in the sunbeam, with my suit flowing around me like a tail, and the novelist said: 'Why did I change?' and I answered with a yawn, for truly I did not care, but ventured that I expected it was all to do with the state of the modern world and man's alienation from man, somehow. When I woke from this uneasy dream, I was as you see me now, and the howls of inmates echoed around me."

"As a psychiatrist, you could not offer some insight into your own dream?"

"Psychiatry is a dog's profession, not a cat's—a cat thinks what he thinks and that is all. He does not worry himself about it, and whatever he thinks, that is the most appropriate and, indeed, excellent thought for a cat to have at that moment. You must understand that each cat is in essence a psychopathology all his own, quite capable of any crime a man could imagine, limited only in size and opposable thumbs; lacking these, we simply connect thought to deed without any intervening neuroses: What we desire, we perform, and that is what is meant by freedom. A dog, on the other hand, wishes to be approved of, by other dogs and by his master, and thus it is the dog who must constantly analyze the motivations and internal mechanisms of others and change his behavior to suit them. Once I was a cat I understood this immediately and forswore my former profession as useless and really rather beneath me. But if you would force me to interpret it, I would tell you that men fear they are monsters at their core, that the civilized skin covers only hideousness and hunger for mire and waste, a driving hunger for death, for rot, for everything that is the opposite of beauty; however, cats know they are monsters and have no particular qualms about it, and besides, their monstrous souls are hidden within an extremely adorable disguise, and few would ever suspect what lies beneath fluffy paws and a fat little belly. Thus cats are not tortured by the idea that one day their insides might be shown to all the world, their fine waistcoats revealed a lie and all for naught. But when I was a man, this was a thing I feared: that I had always been a creature of the dark, only one day having managed to pull on a man's mask, with the certainty therefore that I would be caught out eventually. But I really am tired now and not a little bored, so I believe that's enough for one day. We can take our leave of each other, for the time being at least. I expect you'll want to go back home now, won't you?"

"To my family?" Gregor asked. "I thought I was under arrest." He said this with a certain amount of defiance because, although his friendship had not been accepted, he was feeling more and more independent of all these other cats, especially since Josef K had not reappeared. Surely he was being played with. "How can I go back home when I'm under arrest—indeed, tried and convicted?"

"I see you've misunderstood me," said Franz, who had begun to settle down into a nap, hunching his body so that his shape resembled nothing so much as a roasted chicken. "It's true that you're under arrest, but that shouldn't stop you from carrying out your affairs. And there shouldn't be anything to stop you getting on with your usual life."

"In that case it's not too bad, being under arrest," Gregor said, and crept up close to Franz, sniffing at his pink nose to catch the scent of truth from him, or the scent of a trap being laid, such as telling him he was free to go when in fact he was not and would be immediately chased down by the other cats and tried doubly for some *other* crime he knew not and would not be told, on top of desertion and trying to escape.

"We never meant that it should be anything else," Franz replied.

"It hardly seems to have been necessary to notify me of

the arrest, in that case, or even hold the trial, or bring me here at all," Gregor said, and approached even closer. A few other cats, calicos and blues, mostly, had also come closer. All of them gathered into a narrow space by the door to see what Gregor might say.

"That was my duty," said Franz, his eyes serenely shut.

"A silly duty," said Gregor, unyielding.

"Maybe so," Franz replied, "only don't let's waste our time carrying on like this. I had assumed you'd be wanting to go home. Since you're paying such close attention to every word, I'll add this: I'm not forcing you to go home, I'd just assumed you wanted to. After all, you stayed in that place no matter how unpleasant it was to you before, even letting that unthinkable and rather gauche strap remain around your neck, and perhaps you've now sown your oats and had your adventures on the town and are ready to be a house cat once more, as you were really never anything else. And to make things easier for you, and to let you get home with as little fuss as possible, I've put these three gentle-cats—colleagues of yours, I think—at your disposal."

"What's that?" Gregor exclaimed, and looked at the three in astonishment. He could only remember seeing them in hallways or during holidays when other tenants brought their pets to various celebrations, but these ginger, well-fed young cats were indeed house pets from his building—not *colleagues* of his, that was putting it too high and it showed a gap in Franz's understanding of him, but they were nonetheless about and underfoot from time to time, and he remembered them. He even recalled their odd names: Rabensteiner, with his stiff demeanor and bushy orange tail; Kullich, with his blonde fur; and Kaminer, with his involuntary grin caused by white patterns on his grey muzzle and cheeks. "Good evening," Gregor finally said, extending his paw somewhat ridiculously to the other cats as they yawned in his direction. "I didn't recognize you at all. So, we'll go home now, shall we?" The cats sniggered and nodded enthusiastically, as if that was what they had been waiting for all the time, except that Gregor had not given them leave to go, but now that he had, they felt eager to be off. Gregor sat where he was, thumping his tail back and forth, and watched them squeeze through the opening in the wall they had all come through before the trial; the last to go, of course, was the apathetic Rabensteiner, who had broken into no more than an elegant trot. Kaminer got a bit of mold in his fur, and Gregor, as he'd often had to do when he encountered the tom in the hallway, forcibly reminded himself that the cat's grin was not deliberate, that in fact he wasn't able to grin deliberately.

Once they had gone, Gregor began to quiver and shake with confusion and trepidation. He did not wish to go home— had he not escaped with alacrity?—and further distress his family, yet he felt these narrow-eyed cats had carved up his heart for their plates and left him with no particular idea of anything in the world, sense or nonsense, and it was really very rude to do that to a fellow; in fact, Gregor felt that if one did that, one then had some sort of responsibility for that fellow, and Josef K having gone off to enjoy cream and herring and a harem or whatever his particular peccadilloes might be, that responsibility seemed very clearly to fall to Franz, and Gregor meant to hold him to it, though really the other three could fall off a bridge, so little did he care what befell them now that they were out of the warren and trotting along home to Mrs. Grubach's warm and comfortable lap and also very likely a couple of chicken livers or a bit of sausage.

"So," Gregor called out, kneading his paws against the ground as if this sudden realization needed more room, and addressing all the straggler cats who had come to view his misery, "all of you are working for this organization; I see now that you are all the very bunch of cheats and liars symbolized by the cockroaches in Franz's dream, for you've all pressed yourselves in here to listen in and snoop on me, though you gave the impression of having formed into a proper trial, with factions and arguments, with some of you being for Josef K and some of you for decency and breakfast! Well, I hope you haven't come here for nothing, I hope you've had some fun—let me go or I'll bite you," he shouted to a quivery old Persian who had pressed himself especially close to him—"or else that you've actually learned something. And so I wish you good luck in your vicious legal trade." He briskly wiggled his paw where some bit of filth had gotten stuck to it, surrounded by a silence caused perhaps by the completeness of their surprise. However, the herd of cats seemed to move even more quickly than Gregor, for now they were pressing in even closer—*now*, when he tried to leave, as they had said he could!

"One moment," Franz said without opening his eyes, his unperturbed countenance quite like a sphinx. Gregor stood where he was but looked at his own paws, rather than at his jailor. "I merely wanted to draw your attention," said Franz, "to something you seem not yet to be aware of: no one is keeping you here, nor should anyone have a wish to. In fact, we want nothing at all from you. We belong to the court of the cats, so why would we want anything from you? The court doesn't want anything from you. It accepts you when you come, and it lets you go when you leave." Behind him, the noise of the assembly rose as it became lively once more—probably, Gregor thought, beginning to discuss these events as if making a scientific study of them. "But wherever you go, you will carry with you the knowledge that you are a convict, and your execution shall be just that: the execution of your respectable self, as a cat or a man, and its replacement with a criminal mind, a dark and sneaky place. It's a remarkable apparatus." Franz slitted his eyes open; it appeared that he had responded to Gregor's speech only out of politeness, when he had been just about ready to descend into a highly satisfactory nap. Interest in this execution was not really very high even among the members of the court. Here in the small, deep, underground warren, closed in on all sides by furry bodies, Samsa wore an expression of such doglike resignation that it quite offended the cats, who were accustomed to a certain level of personal pride, whereas Gregor was beginning to look as if one could set him free to roam around the slopes and would only have to whistle at the start of the execution for him to return.

"But why would I return home?" Gregor said with much unhappiness. "The tenor of my family will not have changed in the smallest amount toward me, nor will they be any better off financially or spiritually for my presence. My sister will still torment me with her attentions, my father will refuse to acknowledge me, my mother will weep when she sees me, and my landlord will still demand the rent. And I will have *nothing*, nothing for any of them. Sooner or later my father will put me out on the street in desperation—or worse, throw me in a sack and drown me in the river, sell me to a circus run by some flea-bitten madman, or simply club my head in; and he will not mean it badly—I do not mean to sound like an ungrateful son—but he will be fully within his rights, and I within his power as, yes, you are right, I have always been. But that seems unlikely to change now, and so it seems to me that to return home is to die, to commit myself to my own death, which I suppose is an execution after all, but I still have no real idea what I have been convicted of, unless it is to have been an unhappy man and to have gotten no better as a cat, which I think you know is not an actionable offense; though the tabby Josef K said that the cat stands on the threshold between life and death, surely you cannot mean me to choose to die, to choose to return to that apartment where death surely awaits me in one form or other." Gregor was pleased at the tension among all the people there as they listened to him; a rustling rose from the silence, which was more invigorating than the most ecstatic applause could have been. "There is no doubt," he said quietly, "that there is some enormous organization of cats determining what is said by all of us here. In my case, this includes my prosecution and even what I am saying now, which I suppose constitutes my defense—an organization that employs large muscular cats as intimidators, long-winded tabbies who call themselves bank clerks and judges of whom nothing better can be said than that they are not as arrogant as some house cats I have known in my life. And what, gentlecats, is the purpose of this enormous organization? Its purpose is to arrest innocent kittens and wage pointless prosecutions against them that, as in my case, lead to no result. And then to send them home with an invisible noose around their necks or at least their minds— send them home to die. How are we to avoid cats as a nation becoming deeply corrupt when everything is devoid of meaning? When a man may dream of a novelist and wake up a cat and then be expected to draw some meaning out of it all that is not a colossal joke, that is any more than a photograph of that poor cat with some amusing headline written beneath it for fools to cackle at? It is all for amusement, and that is why innocent, humble cats who never bothered anyone are humiliated in front of crowds rather than being given a proper trial—as if a proper trial is possible when there has been no crime!"

Franz licked his paw and then wiped his left ear thoroughly, which in that dancing language Josef K described seemed to communicate total uncaring for Gregor's accusations or the idea that he might die. "And so what did you dream of, the night you transformed, Gregor S?"

"I cannot recall—I cannot recall, and you cannot force me. But it was nothing like your mad dream, Franz, nothing at all, of that I am sure!" But his body gave lie to his words, and Gregor Samsa's skinny legs twitched, his ears flicked, and before he knew it he was telling his dream in the same musical dance that the other cats knew well. "But yes, yes, I do think there was something, tickling at the back of my mind—I dreamed, I think, that a strange cat was standing before me; I did not feel hungry but rather filled with strength, and it seemed to me that my limbs were light and agile, though I made no attempt to prove this by getting to my feet. A beautiful but not at all extraordinary cat stood before me, I could see that, but that was all, and yet it seemed to me that I saw something more in her. There was blood under me, I soon realized, and at first I took it for food, but I then recognized it as blood that I had vomited. I turned my eyes to the strange cat: She was lean, long legged, brown, with a patch of white here and there, and she had a fine, strong, piercing glance. 'What are you doing here?' she asked. 'You must leave!'

"'I can't leave just now,' I said, without trying to explain, for how could I explain anything to her when she was just a thing in my dream to begin with, and besides she seemed in a hurry. 'Please go,' she said impatiently, lifting her feet and setting them down again. 'Let me be,' I said, 'leave me alone and don't worry about me. No one else worries about me.' 'It's for your own sake,' the cat said. 'You can ask for any sake you like,' I replied, 'I can't go, even if I wanted to. This is my place.' She set about yawning hugely. 'You can go all right, if you choose. It's because you seem to be feeble and a bit of a mess that I ask you now, for you can go now if you like. If you linger, you'll have to run later on.' 'That's my business,' I replied. 'It's mine, too,' she said, saddened by my stubbornness yet obviously resolved to let me be for the time being.

"In the waking world, I would have happily submitted to the blandishments of such a beautiful creature, but at that moment—*why*, I could not tell—the thought of it filled me with terror. 'Get out!' I screamed, and all the louder, for I had no other means of protecting myself. 'But don't I please you?' she asked. 'You'll please me by going away and leaving me in peace,' I said, but I was no longer as sure of myself as I tried to make her think. My senses, sharpened by dreaming and, perhaps a little, by the first beginnings of catlike ways of knowing, suddenly seemed to see or hear something about her: I knew that this cat had the power to drive me, to move me, to destroy me or save me, though I could not at that moment even imagine getting to my own feet. And I gazed at her—she had merely shaken her furry head at my rough answer—with ever-mounting desire. 'Who are you?' I asked. 'I'm a hunter,' she replied. 'And why won't you just let me lie here?' I asked. 'You disturbed me,' she said. 'I can't hunt while you're here.' 'Try,' I said, 'perhaps you'll be able to after all.' 'No,' she said, 'I'm sorry, but you must go.' 'Don't hunt for this one night! Give up hunting entirely! Devote yourself to some other life,' I implored her. 'No,' she said,

'I must hunt.'

"'You must hunt, I must go, nothing but musts,' I said. 'Can you explain to me why we must?' 'No,' she replied, 'but there's nothing that needs to be explained; everything is natural and self-evident.' 'Not so self-evident as all that,' I said. 'You're sorry that you must drive me out of my own dream, yet you do it.' 'That's so,' she replied. 'That's so,' I echoed crassly. 'That isn't an answer. Which sacrifice would you rather make: to give up your hunting or to give up driving me away?' 'To give up my hunting,' she said without hesitation. 'There!' said I. 'Don't you see you're contradicting yourself?' 'How am I contradicting myself?' she replied. 'My dear little kitten'—and I noticed she called me a kitten but had no comprehension of its future meaning—'can it be that you really do not understand that I must? Don't you understand that most obvious fact?' I made no answer, but I noticed—and new life ran through me such as terror brings—I noticed from almost invisible indications the very thing Josef K taught me to see in a cat's body, but which then I understood only by instinct, that in the depths of her chest she was preparing to upraise a kind of song. 'You're going to sing,' I said gravely. 'Yes,' she replied. 'I'm going to sing soon, but not yet.' 'You're beginning already,' I said. 'No,' she said, 'not yet. But be prepared.' 'I can hear it already!' I said, trembling. She was silent, and then I thought I saw something such as no

"I DREAMED, I THINK, THAT A STRANGE AND BEAUTIFUL CAT
WAS STANDING BEFORE ME."

man or cat before me had ever seen, at least there is no slightest hint of it in our histories, and I hastily bowed my head in infinite fear and shame and love and desire in the pool of blood I was lying in. I thought I saw that the cat was already singing without knowing it; nay, more, that the melody, separated from her, floated on the air in accordance with its own law, and, as though she were finished with it and wanted no further part in it, it was moving toward me and me alone. Her song and the blood seeped into me, and I woke and could not remember the dream before now, but I am full of it as I speak to you, Franz, and I remember that great cat and how she spoke to me as though, if I did not depart my own dream, she might hunt me herself. And I wonder if she was not death and misery come home to catch me, and I refused it."

"Perhaps, then," said Franz, "returning home with your conviction hanging on your neck would be like embracing the cat of your dream, the cat of your death, knowing how it all must come out and taking it up anyway; perhaps when we say your current state is a symbol, we mean only that you meant to kill yourself and this is your anxious dream, all of us and your trial and Josef K, and by going to your family you will complete it all and satisfy the novelist of *my* dream, who wants only neat and beautiful endings, where men become monsters and monsters become men."

Franz sauntered away, leaving the way open into the street, and the other cats drew back from Gregor, who wept bitterly and clawed the earth as he exited the court of the cats as if, even as he drew on, he wished to hold himself back for just a few moments more.

# V.

So Gregor Samsa set off to return to the house he had known all his life, and as he saw the willow tree just outside his family's window and caught sight therein of the parlor he had hoped to escape forever, he could feel the apartment looming before him like that same great cat—promising a hunt, and probably death. Why did he not run? He could glimpse his sister within the windows, moving in her morning duties, and he could not think but that he was tired, and nothing seemed sweet anymore, and though he did not know why they had convicted him, surely in his heart he did know he was worthy of conviction, and that his old apartment held his punishment.

"Look at her," Gregor thought to himself as he watched his sister within, "she is grown into a little woman now, quite slim, yet she is tightly laced as well. She is always in the same dress I see, having had to sell her others; look at it, how like fur it seems from this distance, it being made of dark grey stuff, something like the color of Josef K, and trimmed discreetly with tassels or buttonlike hangings of the same color. She never wears a hat any longer, her dull fair hair is smooth and not untidy, though, but worn very loose." Gregor noted that although his sister was tightly laced, she was quick and light in her movements—actually rather overdoing the quickness, as if afraid to discover their mother or father changed in the fashion of Gregor, running about under her feet—putting her hands on her hips and abruptly turning the upper part of her body sideways with a surprising suddenness. The impression her hand had always made on Gregor could only be conveyed by saying that he had never seen a hand so eager to stroke and to scratch, to imprison and impugn on his dignity. Yet it was not peculiar or ugly, but a normal and nearly lovely hand, one he had once been fond of.

"This little woman," Gregor thought then, "is very ill-pleased with me, even if she doesn't know at all where I have been, and even before my situation she always found something to object to—I was always doing the wrong thing, home too often or away too long—a true daughter of our mother and father, and now I annoy her with every step. If a life could be cut into the smallest of small pieces and every scrap of it could be separately assessed, every scrap of my current life would now be objectionable to her, save that scrap of me that was once her brother and her bill payer. And yet if I had only been a better cat, I could have endured her attentions when she wished to give them to me; but now she will want nothing of them, having had a space without me, time to feel relief and wonder at how she ever tolerated my antics. Like a wife whose husband has strayed, she will find only fault in my person from here on out because I have scorned her petting and, worse, run away. But I wonder now how I can be such an offense to her; it cannot be that anything about me enrages her sense of beauty—I am a fine enough cat, I have pleasant fur when I do not need brushing, my nose is quite pink, and I have a tail the equal of anyone's. But perhaps I enrage her feeling for justice, her habits, her traditions, her hopes for the future, and our now completely incompatible natures—or at least my nature is incompatible with her hopes and her taste in collars. And perhaps it is because I have now grown much larger than a usual cat, just as Josef K and Franz and Willem did—there is something within our former natures as men that wishes to swell the feline form to our own original proportions. But, really, all she has to do is regard me as an utter stranger, a pet she discovered in a shop or an alley; indeed, I should welcome this situation, and she and the rest need only forget my existence, save for food in the mornings and evenings and all their—and my!—torments would be at an end. I am not even thinking of myself, I am quite leaving out of the account the fact that I find it all very trying, leaving it out because I recognize my discomfort is small compared to the suffering she endures. All the same, I am well aware that hers will no longer be an affectionate suffering—she has left off, I can see, seeking any improvement for me, building a little door for me into the kitchen or tidying up my sand-box, for she does not care about my development, only for her own personal interest in the matter, which I admit is large, and perhaps she will be keen to visit on me revenge for the torments I have given her. I have already tried once to effect the best way of putting a stop to all this perpetual misery, which is to say I absented myself, but my very attempts brought me down to such a nadir of misery that I shall not repeat it. No, I am convicted, that is all."

He felt, too, a certain responsibility laid upon him, if you like to put it that way, for the strangers they were now to each other, his sister and himself, and however true it was that one day soon the sole connection between them would be the vexation he caused her, or rather the vexation she let him cause her, and Gregor reminded himself that he ought not to feel indifferent to the visible physical suffering that this induced in her. Every morning, before he escaped and, he presumed, today as well, she rose a bit paler, more unslept; their mother was frequently worrying about her, wondering what could have caused her condition, if not Gregor's unhappy shape, and no other answer was to be found: Grete's vexation, soon to be daily renewed, lay with her brother. "True," Gregor thought, "I am not so worried about her as the rest of my family, for she is hardy and tough; anyone who is capable of such strong feeling is likely also to be capable of surviving its effects. I have even a suspicion that her sufferings—or some of them, at least—are only a pretense to bring me willingly into her arms. She is too kind to admit openly what a torment my very existence is to her; to discuss in public this unclean affliction of hers would be too shameful. But to keep utterly silent about something that so persistently rankles will soon also be too much for her. So with feminine guile she steers a middle course; she keeps silent but betrays all the outward signs of a secret sorrow in order to draw gentle attention to the matter. Perhaps she even hopes that public attention will be paid to me, that the press should be alerted and doctors, too, and a general public rancor against me might rise up and use all its great powers to condemn me definitively to dissection, much more effectively and quickly than her relatively feeble private rancor could do; she would then retire into the background, draw a breath of relief, and turn her back on me. Well, if that is what she hopes, she is deluding herself. The cats have already decided I am guilty of, well, being guilty, and public opinion would never find me as infinitely objectionable as my own family can, even under its most powerful magnifying glass. I am not so altogether useless a creature as she thinks; I don't want to boast, and especially not in this connection; but if I am not conspicuous for specially useful qualities such as earning income, I am certainly not conspicuous for the lack of others such as mousing; only to her, only to her these days almost bleached eyes, do I appear so. So in this respect I can feel quite reassured, can I? She will accept me and love me once more? No, not at all; for if it becomes generally known that my situation is making her positively ill, the world should put questions to me that I could not answer except for my helpless meowing: Why am I tormenting the poor little woman with my incorrigible refusal to return to my previous human station, and do I mean to drive her to her death, and my mother, too, and when am I going to show some sense and have enough decent human feeling to stop such goings-on, do away with myself for the decency of my family? If the world were to ask me that, it would be difficult to find an answer. Should I admit frankly that I don't much believe in anything anymore and thus produce the unfavorable impression of being a man who has divested himself of connections, and in such an ungallant manner? And how could I say that she would be better off without me entirely, which is to say with me being dead; I should not feel the slightest sympathy for her subsequent grief, since she made herself a complete nuisance to me and any connection between us is summed up by the ridiculous belled collar she fitted me with? I don't say that people wouldn't believe me; they would be interested enough in the strange tale to get so far as belief; they would simply note the ungrateful adjectives I used concerning such a frail, sick girl, and that would be little in my favor. Any answer I made would inevitably come up against the world's incapacity to keep down the suspicion that there must be black magic behind such a case as this, and that if such a thing existed it would hardly come from me, since I scarcely have benefitted from the whole affair! Grete, at any rate, shows not a trace of grief concerning my absence, nor will she show any kindness toward me anymore that I can see; therein would lie my last hope for love—that her old habit might resurface and, out of accustomed loving, new love might arise. But if any of it got out, public opinion, which is wholly insensitive in such matters, would of course abide by its prejudices and denounce me.

"So the only thing left for me to do would be to hope that my old balding head and gouty leg might emerge again from

this furry body, that I might heal before the world could intervene, which might be sufficient to lessen my family's rancor—
not to wean them from it altogether, naturally, which would be
unthinkable after all that has passed. And, indeed, I have often
asked myself if I am pleased enough with my present self to be
unwilling to change it, and whether I could not attempt some
changes in myself, even so far as the power of speech to explain
my state or scratching letters in the carpet. Her objection to
me, as I am now aware, is a fundamental one, and rightly so;
nothing can remove it, not even the removal of myself. If she
heard that I had committed suicide, she would fall into a fit of
helpless rage against me who left her in such straits.

"Now I cannot imagine that such a sharp-witted woman
as she does not understand as well as I do both the hopelessness
of her own state and the helplessness of mine, my inability, with
the best will in the world, to conform to her requirements. I am
now a cat. I am helpless to be otherwise. Of course she under-
stands it, but being a fighter by nature, she forgets it in the lust
of battle, and in my unfortunate disposition I cannot help, because in any case it is my nature to purr gently at anyone who
flies into a violent passion. In this way, naturally, we shall never
come to terms. I wish I could but depart all and everything at
once and never have to face her more, to disappoint her ambitions and show by the very presence of my grotesque and

growing body how little she now has to look forward to in the world.

"But on the contrary, such a self-immolation is just what I must avoid; if I am to follow a course of action at all it must be that of keeping the affair within its present narrow limits, growing not too much fatter or silkier, and most certainly not to involve the outside world; that is to say, I must stay quietly where I am and not let it affect my heart as far as can be seen, and that includes being sure my sister mentions it to no one, because it is a kind of dangerous mystery. But I must pretend it is a trivial, purely familial matter and as such to be hidden and to be kept to ourselves."

Gregor wriggled himself into a position to leap upon the window sash and slip in, for it remained open. "I am less upset by the situation," he thought, "now that I think I perceive how unlikely it is to come to any sort of definitive crisis; imminent as it often seems to be, one is eagerly disposed—when one is young and, especially, when one is female—to exaggerate the speed with which crises arrive. Things will go on as they have been, I've no doubt. Whenever Grete shall grow faint at the very sight of me, I shall sink adorably sideways into a chair, plucking playfully at her bodice strings with my paws while tears of rage and despair roll down her cheeks, and I shall make her laugh and cheer her. I shall always think the moment has now come, that I am on the point of being summoned to an-swer as best I can for myself and banished forever. And yet it will not have come. They are family and must endure me; I shall live here until I am an old tom, and they must care for me. Youth casts a bloom of urgency over everything; our more awk-ward characteristics such as tails and whiskers seem stark in the upswell of youthful energy. If, as a youth, a man is a cat, it may be counted against him; but as an old man it is not even noticed, not even by himself, for the things that survive in old age are necessary and may grow to be appreciated. Everyone says: yes, he has always been a cat, the old monster, but there's a charm in him. In the end, it will all be all right, I know it. I know it. I shall continue to live my own life for a long time to come, un-troubled by the world, despite all the outbursts of my family; I shall bear it all with ease, and be petted, and be given another pretty bell for my collar. I know this is how it shall proceed."

The windowsill was cold under Gregor's paws, but he en-dured it.

Slipping back into the house with the breaking of dawn, Gregor remembered clearly his last impression the previous evening: that his father had badly misunderstood Grete's plea for help upon his escape and assumed that Gregor had committed some violence upon his mother. It seemed impossible that so little time had passed since that moment, and yet it was so, only a night, and now nearly morning. Thus, Gregor now had to calm his father straightaway, before breakfast, for yesterday he had neither the time nor the ability to explain things. And so he rushed through the parlor to the door of his own room and pushed himself against it, his furry bulk now really quite substantial, so that his father—who, Gregor saw as he crossed the floor, was already awake, sitting right there at the table—could see right away that Gregor fully intended to return humbly to the familiar state of things, that it was not necessary to force him into his room, but that one only needed to open the door, and he would disappear therein immediately.

But his father was not in the mood to observe such niceties. "Ah," he yelled as soon as he saw Gregor, with a tone as if he were all at once angry and pleased. Gregor pulled his head back from the door and raised it in the direction of his father, his eyes as large and sweet as he could make them. The terror of remembering his dream and the other cats' conviction still clung to him, and his only hope, he felt, was to make his family love him once more, to pet him and care for him as Mrs. Grubach did her cats, and of course he would even tolerate Grete's attentions if it meant everything could return to the way it had been—after all, had they not always kept him as a kind of pet, one who gave them money, and in return they tolerated him? That was all he asked, to be tolerated again.

He had not really pictured his father waiting for him immediately upon his return; Gregor had hoped to have time to organize his strategies. Of course, he now realized, after all this time he had spent huddled, four-legged and furry, in his room, he really should have grasped the fact that he would encounter different conditions in the apartment, especially now that his family had had a night to think themselves free of him and begin planning for the future. Nevertheless, nevertheless— it had been long weeks until now since he had seen his father with his own eyes; was this really his father? This man who, in earlier days, had lain exhausted in bed whenever Gregor was setting out on a business trip; who had received him on the evenings of his return in a sleeping gown and armchair, totally incapable of standing up; whose only sign of approval would be to lift his arm a bit; who, during their rare family strolls a few Sundays a year and on the important holidays, made his way slowly forward between Gregor and his mother, who themselves moved slowly, but he always a bit *more* slowly, bundled up in his old coat, all the time setting down his walking stick carefully; and who, when he had wanted to say something, almost always stood still and gathered his entourage around him? In that instant Gregor felt a kind of boiling feline contempt rise in him; even a cat napping away an afternoon was less useless and lazy than all that.

But now his father rose from his seat, standing up really straight, already dressed for the day in a tight-fitting blue uniform with gold buttons, like the ones worn by bank employees. Above the high stiff collar of his jacket, his firm double chin stuck out prominently; beneath his bushy eyebrows the glance of his black eyes was freshly penetrating and alert, and his otherwise disheveled white hair was combed down into a carefully exact shining part. He threw his cap—on which a gold monogram, apparently the symbol of the bank, was affixed—in an arc all the way across the room onto the sofa, and flipping back the edge of the long coat of his uniform with a grim face, he stepped right up to Gregor.

Gregor really didn't know what his father had in mind, but now the man raised his foot uncommonly high, and Gregor was astonished at the gigantic size of the sole of his boot. However, he did not linger on that point, for he recalled from the first day of his new life that, as far as he was concerned, his father considered the greatest force the only appropriate response. And it seemed that finding him returned to the house now, after they had surely all taken a breath of relief upon deciding him gone, had not improved his father's disposition. So Gregor scurried quickly away from his father, sliding on the polished floors; he stopped when his father remained standing in place and then scampered forward again when his father so much as stirred.

In this way they made their way round and round the room, without anything decisive taking place; because of their stop-and-start progress, it didn't look precisely like a chase, more like the sort of game a dog would enjoy, though a cat does not. Gregor remained on the floor for the time being, especially since he was afraid that his father would interpret jumping onto the draperies or the bookcases as an act of real malice. In any case, Gregor was forced to admit to himself that he couldn't keep up this running around for a long time, that in fact it was all worse than before—and worse even than being caught by the cats, because whenever his father took a single step, Gregor had to rush through an enormous number of movements, his paws scrabbling on the floor as he frantically sought a new haven. Already he was starting to suffer from a shortage of breath, just as in his earlier days when his lungs had been quite unreliable, and besides he had been up without sleep all night.

As he now began to stagger in place, trying to gather all his energies to continue running but having trouble keeping his eyes open, feeling so exhausted of mind that he could form no notion of any plan for escape besides running and had already all but forgotten that the window was still available to him—at that moment something flew through the air, smacking down onto the ground in front of him and rolling right past. It was an apple. Immediately a second one flew after it. Gregor stood still in fright: further running away was useless, for his father had decided to bombard him.

From the fruit bowl on the sideboard his father had filled his pockets. And now, for the moment not bothering to take accurate aim, he was throwing apple after apple. These small red orbs rolled around on the floor, colliding with one another as if doing battle. A weakly thrown apple grazed Gregor's back but skidded off harmlessly. Then, running out of fruit but with his fury still unabated, Gregor's father promptly grabbed and threw the next fist-size thing within reach, which was a ball of yarn that Gregor's sister had been saving to knit a winter scarf for herself. It brushed harmlessly against Gregor's ear, but then abruptly he yowled as he felt his head jerk tight; a loop of yarn had caught the latch of his collar, which now was pulling at his neck painfully.

Gregor wanted to drag himself away, as if he could leave behind the unexpected and incredible pain simply by moving from the spot where it had struck him. But he felt as if he was nailed in place; he lay stretched out, completely confused in all his senses. Only with luck did he glance across the room and notice that the door of his room had been pulled open, and that right in front of his sister, who was yelling, his mother ran out in her undergarments—for his sister had undressed her in order to give her some freedom to breathe amid her fainting spell, and thus had she gone to bed—his mother ran up to his father, her skirts falling to the floor one after the other, tripping her as she hurled herself onto his father, throwing her arms around his neck and seeming to melt completely into his body as she begged him to spare Gregor's life—and at this moment Gregor's vision began to blur and fade.

How quickly it had all happened, he thought as he stumbled toward his room. Franz was right. He was always meant to die here.

# VI.

Gregor's labored breathing, from which he had now suffered for over a month—he had managed to chew off the ball of yarn, but a short length remained unreachably twisted in his collar, invisible to all beneath his tufting fur yet continuing as he grew larger and larger to pull the collar alarmingly tight against his throat—seemed by itself to have reminded his father that, in spite of Gregor's inexplicable and often undignified appearance, Gregor was a member of the family, not a thing to be treated as an enemy, and that it was, on the contrary, a requirement of family duty to suppress one's aversion to a son who could lick his hindquarters with acrobatic ease, and to endure—nothing else, just endure. And if, through his afflicted throat and tightened breath, Gregor had now apparently lost for good his ability to move with any ease, and for the time being needed many long minutes to crawl across his room, like an aged invalid—climbing up high, of course, had become unimaginable—nevertheless, he felt that for this worsening of his condition he was compensated satisfactorily, because every day toward evening, the door to the living room, on which he was now in the habit of keeping a sharp eye for an hour or two beforehand, was opened, so that he, lying down in the darkness of his room, invisible from the living room, could see the entire family at the illuminated table and listen to their conversation with, to at least some extent, their permission—a situation quite improved from what had been the arrangement before.

Of course, there was no longer the lively socializing of years gone by, which Gregor had used to think about in small hotel rooms with a certain longing, when, tired out, he had been prone to throw himself upon damp bedclothes. What went on now was, for the most part, very quiet. After the evening meal, Gregor's father fell asleep quickly in his armchair. His mother and sister talked mutedly in the stillness while his mother, hunching over, worked at sewing fine undergarments for a fashion shop. Grete, who had taken on a job as a salesgirl, studied stenography and French in the evening, so as perhaps

GREGOR'S LABORED BREATHING SEEMED TO HAVE REMINDED HIS FATHER
THAT HE WAS A MEMBER OF THE FAMILY.

later to obtain a better position. Sometimes their father woke up and, as if quite unaware that he had been sleeping, said to their mother, "How long you have been sewing today?" and went right back to sleep, leaving Grete and their mother to smile tiredly at one another.

With a determined stubbornness, Gregor's father refused to take off his bank uniform even at home; his sleeping gown hung on the coat hook, unused, while he dozed off still completely dressed, as if he need always be ready to leap to his duties and even here might be summoned by the voice of his superior. As a result, in spite of all the care given by Gregor's mother and sister, his father's uniform, which even at first had not been new, grew dirty, and Gregor often spent the entire evening staring at the outfit—stains all over it, though its gold buttons were always polished—in which the old man, uncomfortable though he must be, nonetheless slept peacefully.

As soon as the clock struck ten, Gregor's mother tried gently encouraging his father to wake up and go to bed, telling him that he couldn't sleep properly in his chair and that, since he had to report to work at six o'clock, he really needed a good sleep. But with the obstinacy that had gripped him since he had returned to the workforce, his father invariably insisted on continuing to lounge even longer at the table. No matter how much Gregor's mother and sister might plead with him, for a quarter of an hour his father would just keep shaking his head slowly, his eyes closed, without standing up. Gregor's mother would pull him by the sleeve and speak cajoling words into his ear, and his sister would set down her work to try and help, but nothing worked; Gregor's father would just settle down more deeply still into his chair. Only when the two women together leaned forward and grabbed him under the armpits would he throw open his eyes, look back and forth between them, and say, "This is the life. This is the peace and quiet of my old age." Propped up by both women, he would heave himself up elaborately as if it was a tremendous trouble for him, allow himself to be led to the door, wave the women away there and proceed on his own, though Gregor's mother had put down her sewing implements and his sister her pen in order to go after him and help him some more. "Perhaps," Gregor once thought he heard his father say, "we should get a little kitten, to keep us company."

In this overworked and exhausted family, who had time to worry any longer about Gregor—at least, more than was absolutely necessary? The servant girl, of course, had been let go, and so a huge, bony cleaning woman with white hair flying all around her head came every morning and evening to do the heaviest housework; Gregor's mother took care of everything else in addition to her considerable sewing work. It even happened that numerous pieces of the family jewelry, which Gregor's mother and sister had always been so happy to wear on social and festive occasions, were sold, as Gregor learned from overhearing general discussion about the prices they had fetched. But the family's greatest complaint was always that they could not leave this apartment, which was too big for their present means, since they could imagine no way in which Gregor might be moved. Yet Gregor recognized that it was not just consideration for him that was preventing such a move, for he could have been transported easily enough in a large box with a few air holes and perhaps a saucer of milk. No, the main thing holding them all back from relocating to more affordable living quarters was their complete sense of hopelessness, their despair over the idea that they had been struck by a misfortune the likes of which had been suffered by no one else in their entire circle of relatives and acquaintances.

Gregor's household, therefore, now took up in earnest the poor family's lot in life. His father brought breakfast to the petty officials at the bank; his mother sacrificed herself for the undergarments of strangers; his sister sat at her desk, at the beck and call of customers; but the family's energies could not reach any further. And Gregor's constricted throat began to pain him all over again, especially when mother and sister, after they had escorted his father to bed, would come back to the living room and let their work lie that they might sit close together, cheek to cheek, and his mother would say, pointing to Gregor's room, "Close the door, Grete," leaving Gregor again in the darkness, while nearby he understood the women were mingling their tears, or, quite dry eyed, staring at the table.

Gregor barely slept now, nights or days. Sometimes he imagined that the next time the door opened, he would take over the family arrangements just as he had before. In his day-dreams there began to once again appear the likes of his employer at the sales office, the supervisor and the apprentices, the excessively spineless custodian, two or three friends from other businesses, a chambermaid from a hotel in the provinces—a fleeting memory of love—a girl who worked in a hat shop, whom he had courted seriously but too slowly; they all appeared in his imagination, mixed in with strangers or people he had already forgotten. But instead of helping him and his family, they were all unapproachable, and in the end he was happy to see them disappear.

Other times, he was in no mood to worry about his family. He seethed with fury over the wretched care he was getting, even though he couldn't imagine anything that he might have an appetite for. Still, he made plans about how he could take from the larder all the food he certainly deserved, even if he wasn't hungry. About how he would return to Josef K and

Franz and, depending on how miserable his affliction felt, either show them what a noble cat he could be, how he could hunt with them and be of use to the court, or else claw their eyes out and eat their ears.

Gregor's sister, without thinking anymore about how she might be able to give him any special pleasure, now quickly tossed a bit of food into his room every morning and noon before she ran off to her shop; then in the evening, quite indifferent to whether the food had perhaps only been tasted or, as happened more frequently, remained entirely untouched, she whisked it out with one sweep of her broom. The task of cleaning his room, which she now always carried out in the evening, could not be done any more hurriedly. Streaks of dirt ran along the walls; here and there lay tangles of dust and garbage. At first, when his sister arrived, Gregor would position himself in a particularly filthy corner in hopes of making evident a sort of protest. But he could have well stayed there for weeks without his sister's taking care to do anything differently. She saw the dirt just as clearly as he did—she had decided just to let it stay.

With a pronounced touchiness that was quite new to her, and had in fact generally taken over the entire family, Grete insisted that the upkeep of Gregor's room remained reserved for her alone. Once, just once, his mother had undertaken a major cleaning of the room, which employed the use of several buckets of water. But the extensive dampness made Gregor sick, and he lay supine, embittered and immobile on the couch. His mother's punishment was not delayed for long, in any case, for that evening, as soon as his sister observed the change in Gregor's room, she ran into the living room mightily offended and broke out in a fit of crying, uncaring of her mother's pleading entreaties. Their father, of course, woke up with a start in his chair, and the parents stared at her astonished and helpless, until they, too, started to grow agitated. Turning to Gregor's mother, his father reproached her, ordering that she was not to take over the cleaning of Gregor's room from the sister—and then, turning to Grete on his other side, he shouted that she would no longer be allowed to clean Gregor's room ever again. As he grew increasingly beside himself, Gregor's mother tried to pull his father into their bedroom; meanwhile, Grete, still shaking with her crying fit, pounded on the table with her tiny fists, and Gregor sat and hissed at all this, angry that no one thought about shutting the door and sparing him the sight of such commotion.

As it happened, even after his sister, exhausted from her daily work, had grown tired of caring for Gregor as she used to, even then his mother did not have to take up the burden—and yet Gregor was not neglected. For now the cleaning woman was there. This old widow, who had clearly survived much in her long life with the help of her bony frame, had no real horror of Gregor. Without being in the least curious, she had once by chance opened Gregor's door. At the sight of Gregor— who, totally surprised, began to scamper here and there though no one was chasing him, playing almost as if he were his old self and occupiable with a bit of yarn or mouse—she remained standing with her hands folded across her stomach, staring at him. Since that day, she never failed to open the door furtively a little every morning and evening to look in on Gregor. At first, she also called him to her with words that she presumably thought were friendly, like "Come here for a bit, old kitty!" or "Hey, look at the sweet kitty!" Addressed in such a manner, Gregor answered nothing, but remained motionless in his place, as if the door had not been opened at all. If only, instead of allowing this cleaning woman to disturb him uselessly whenever she felt like it, they had given her orders to clean up his room every day!

One day in the early morning—a hard downpour, perhaps an early sign of the coming spring, struck the window panes— when the cleaning woman started up once again with her usual conversation, Gregor was so bitter that he turned toward her, as if for an attack, arching his back, although slowly and weakly. But instead of reacting with fear, the cleaning woman merely lifted up a chair standing close by the door and, as she stood there with her mouth wide open, her intention was clear: she would close her mouth only when the chair in her hand had been thrown down on Gregor's back. "Enough of this—got it?" she asked, as Gregor turned himself around again, and she placed the chair calmly back in the corner. He was helpless; why did she hate him so, when those ginger cats of Mrs. Grubach's enjoyed the run of the neighborhood, leaping blithely on and off the window sill just outside, as if they'd never been brought to meet him and had no obligation to him at all? Perhaps she had a phobia, or perhaps she needed a good biting to improve her disposition.

GREGOR ATE HARDLY anything anymore. Only when he chanced to walk past the food that had been prepared would he, almost as a game, take a bit into his mouth and make a perfunctory attempt at swallowing before, usually, spitting it out again. At first he thought it might be his sadness over the condition of his room and the loss of all possibilities, the loss of the life he might have had as a street cat, that kept him from eating; but he very soon became reconciled to the new, lessened state of his room and his life. The family and the cleaning woman had grown accustomed to storing in his room things that had no place anywhere else—and at this point there were many such things, now that they had rented one room of the apartment to three lodgers. These solemn gentlemen—all three had full

beards, as Gregor once found out through a crack in the door—
were meticulously intent on tidiness, not only in their own
room but, since they were now living here, in the entire household, and particularly in the kitchen. They simply did not tolerate any useless or shoddy stuff. Moreover, they had brought
along many of their own pieces of furniture. Many of the family's items had thus become superfluous, and these were not really things one could sell or things one wanted to throw out. All
these items, then, ended up in Gregor's room, even the box of
ashes and the garbage pail from the kitchen. The cleaning
woman, always in a hurry, simply flung anything that was momentarily useless into Gregor's room. (Fortunately, Gregor generally saw only the object and the hand that held it.) The
cleaning woman perhaps meant, when time and opportunity
allowed, to take the stuff out again or to eventually dispose of
it all at once, but in fact the mess just remained there, however
it had landed upon being tossed, unless Gregor squirmed his
way through the accumulation of junk and pushed things
around himself. At first he was forced to do this because otherwise there was no room for him to slink around, but later he did
it with a growing pleasure—although after such exertion, tired
to death and feeling wretched, he wouldn't budge for hours.

Because the lodgers sometimes took their evening meal at
home at the common table, the door to the living room now

stayed shut on many evenings. But Gregor had no trouble at all going without the open door. Even on many evenings when it was open he had stopped availing himself of it; without the family noticing, he would instead simply stretch out in the darkest corner of his room. However, one night the cleaning woman left the door to the living room slightly ajar, and it remained open even when the lodgers arrived in the evening and the lights were put on. They sat down at the head of the table where in earlier days his mother, his father, and Gregor had eaten, unfolded their napkins, and picked up their knives and forks. Gregor's mother promptly appeared from the kitchen with a dish of meat; right behind her came his sister carrying a dish piled high with potatoes. The food gave off a lot of steam. The gentlemen lodgers bent over the plates set before them, as if they wanted to examine the meal before eating, and in fact the one who sat in the middle—he seemed to serve as the leader of the three—cut off a piece of meat still on the plate, obviously to establish whether it was sufficiently tender or whether it should be shipped back to the kitchen. He was satisfied, and Gregor's mother and sister, who had looked on in suspense, now breathed easily and smiled.

The family themselves ate in the kitchen. But before Gregor's father went into the kitchen, he came into the common room and with a bow, cap in hand, made a tour of the table. The lodgers rose up collectively and murmured something in their beards. Then, when they were alone, they ate almost in complete silence. It seemed odd to Gregor that, out of all the many different sorts of sounds of eating, what was always audible was their swallowing, as if demonstrating to Gregor that people needed the full use of their throats to eat and nothing productive could be accomplished with even the keenest teeth and tongue alone. "I really do have an appetite," Gregor said to himself sorrowfully, "but not for these things. How these lodgers stuff themselves, and I am starving to death."

On this particular evening, the violin sounded from the kitchen. Gregor couldn't remember having heard it all through this period. The lodgers had by now ended their night meal; the middle one had pulled out a newspaper and handed a page each to the other two, and they were now leaning back, reading and smoking. When the violin started playing, they grew attentive; they got up and went on tiptoe to the kitchen door, at which they remained standing pressed up against one another. They must have been audible from the kitchen, because Gregor's father called out, "Perhaps the gentlemen don't like the playing? It can be stopped at once." "On the contrary," stated the lodger in the middle, "might the young woman not come into us and play in the room here, where it is really much more comfortable and cheerful?" "Oh, thank you!" cried out Gregor's father, as if he were the one playing the violin. The men stepped back into the room and waited. In a moment, Gregor's father emerged with the music stand, his mother with the sheet music, and his sister with the violin. Grete calmly prepared everything for the recital. The parents—who had never before rented out a room and therefore were clearly overdoing their politeness to the lodgers—dared not sit on their own chairs. Gregor's father leaned against the door, his right hand stuck between two buttons of his buttoned-up uniform. The mother, however, accepted a chair offered by one lodger; since she made sure to leave it where the gentleman had chanced to put it, she sat to one side in a corner.

Gregor's sister began to play. His father and mother both followed attentively the movements of her hands. Gregor, attracted by the music, ventured to creep a little farther forward, now poking his head into the living room. He gave little thought to his lack of consideration for the others. Before, he would have taken their presence very seriously and would have felt at this moment all the more reason to hide away, because— as a result of the dust that lay all over his room and flew around with the slightest movement—he was totally covered in dirt. Stuck to his fur all over was dust, thread, hair, and specks of food. His indifference to everything was such that he could no longer be bothered to lie on his back and scratch it on the carpet, as he frequently used to do. Now, in spite of his condition, Gregor felt no timidity about inching forward through his door onto the spotless floor of the living room.

In any case, no one paid him any attention. The family was all caught up in the violin playing. The lodgers, by contrast—who had promptly placed themselves, hands in their trouser pockets, behind the music stand, much too close to Gregor's sister, so that they could all see the sheet music, something that must certainly bother the girl—soon drew back to the window, conversing in low voices with bowed heads, where they remained as Gregor's father worriedly watched them. It seemed clear that their expectation of a beautifully entertaining violin recital had been disappointed, and it was now only out of politeness that they were allowing the continued interruption of their regular peace and quiet. Particularly, the way in which they all blew their cigar smoke out of their noses and mouths led one to conclude that they were quite irritated. And yet Gregor's sister was playing so beautifully. Her face was turned to the side, her gaze followed the score intently and sadly. Gregor crept forward a little farther still, keeping his head close against the floor in order to be able to catch her gaze if possible. Was he fully an animal now, that music so captivated him? And of course it brought to mind the terrible song of the cat of his dreams, and the music of Josef K's seven cats. For him it was as if the way to the unknown nourishment he craved was revealing itself. He was determined to press forward right to his sister, to tug at her dress, and to indicate to her in this way that she might bring her violin into his room and cuddle him and press him to her breast once more. He would not struggle. No one here valued her recital as he did, as he wanted to. He did not wish to let her leave his room ever again, at least not as long as he lived. It occurred to him that his frightening appearance would for the first time become useful for him; he imagined guarding all the doors of his room simultaneously, snarling back at any attackers. Of course, his sister should not be compelled— no, she would remain with him voluntarily. She would sit next to him on the sofa, bend down her ear to him, and he would then confide in her that he absolutely intended to send her to the conservatory, and, indeed, if his misfortune had not arrived in the interim, he would have declared all this last Christmas— had Christmas really already come and gone?—and would have brooked no argument. After this explanation, his sister would break out in tears of emotion, and Gregor would lift himself up to her armpit and kiss her throat, which she, from the time she started going to work, had begun to leave exposed, wearing no ribbon or collar.

"Mr. Samsa," called out the middle lodger to Gregor's father, and, without uttering a further word, pointed his index finger at Gregor, who was creeping slowly forward. The violin fell silent. The middle lodger smiled, first shaking his head once at his friends, and then looked down at Gregor once more. His father, rather than rushing to drive Gregor back again, seemed to consider it of prime importance to calm the lodgers—although they were not acting particularly upset, even though Gregor's size was so great now that he could not fit on the large living room chair, for he would have crushed it entirely; perhaps, indeed, *because* of his size, Gregor seemed to fascinate the lodgers more than the violin recital had. His father hurried over to them and, with outstretched arms, tried to push them into their own room and simultaneously to block their view of Gregor with his own body. At this point they became really somewhat irritated, although it was impossible to tell whether that was because of his father's behavior or because of the dawning realization that they had been living, without know- ing it, alongside a neighbor like Gregor.

They demanded explanations from Gregor's father, raised their arms to make their points, tugged agitatedly at their beards, and moved back toward their room quite slowly. Meanwhile, the utter lack of attention that had suddenly fallen upon Grete after the sudden breaking off of the recital overwhelmed her. She held onto the violin and bow in her limp hands for a little while, continuing to stare at the sheet music as if she was still playing. Then, all at once, she pulled herself together, placed the instrument in her mother's lap—the woman was still sitting in her chair, having trouble breathing, for her lungs were laboring, and Gregor's labored in a mirror of hers, on account of his sister's collar and his father's flung yarn, he wheezed and coughed alongside his mother in distress—and ran into the next room, which the lodgers, pressured by his father, were nearing closer and closer. Gregor could see how, under his sister's practiced hands, the sheets and pillows on the beds were quickly tidied and arranged. Even before the lodgers reached the room, she had finished fixing the beds and slipped out again—which was good, for their father seemed so gripped once again with his stubbornness that he was forgetting to treat his renter with the usual deference and respect. Instead, he pressed on and on until, at the door of the rented room, the middle gentleman stamped loudly with his foot and thus brought Gregor's father to a standstill.

"I hereby declare," the middle lodger said, raising his hand and casting his glance on both Gregor's mother and sister, "that considering the disgraceful conditions prevailing in this apartment and family"—with this he spat decisively on the floor—"I immediately cancel my room. I will, of course, pay nothing at all for the days that I have lived here; on the contrary I shall think about whether or not I will initiate some sort of action against you, something that—believe me—will be very easy to establish." He fell silent and stared, as if he was waiting for something. His two friends suddenly joined in, discovering their own opinions: "We also give immediate notice." At that they stepped into their room; the middle lodger seized the door handle, banged the door shut, and locked it.

How much easier things had been when Gregor was a kitten and small enough to pass, almost, somewhat, for a usual sort of beast who might live in a house.

His father groped his way to his chair and let himself fall in it. It looked as if he were stretching out for his usual evening snooze, but the heavy nodding of his head showed that he was not in fact sleeping at all. Gregor had lain motionless the entire time in the spot where the lodgers had caught him. His disappointment with the collapse of his plan to seduce his sister into loving him once more—and perhaps also weakness brought on by his severe hunger—made it impossible for him to move. He was certainly afraid that a general disaster would break upon him at any moment, and he waited. He was not even startled when the violin fell from his mother's lap, out from under her trembling fingers, and gave off a reverberating tone.

"My dear parents," said Gregor's sister, banging her hand on the table by way of an introduction, "things cannot go on any longer in this way. Maybe if you don't understand that, well,

I do. I will not utter my brother's name in front of this monster, who sits in its own filth and wheezes and almost certainly has fleas and grows so large that soon even his room will not contain him, and thus I say only that we must try to get rid of it. We have tried what is humanly possible to take care of it and to be patient. I am quite sure that no one could possibly criticize us in the slightest."

"She is right. A thousand times she is right," said Gregor's father. His mother, who was still incapable of breathing properly because of the dust and dander, began to cough numbly with her hand held up over her mouth and a manic expression in her eyes. Grete hurried over to her mother and held her forehead.

The girl's words seemed to have led her father to certain reflections. He sat upright, played with his uniform hat among the plates—which still lay on the table from the lodgers' evening meal—and glanced now and then at the motionless Gregor.

"We must get rid of it," Gregor's sister now said decisively to her father, for her mother, in her coughing fit, was not listening to anything. "It is killing you both. I see it coming. When people have to work as hard as we all do, they cannot also tolerate this endless torment at home. Such strangeness, to have a brother who vanished and left only an ungrateful furball in his place. I just can't go on anymore." And she broke out into such a crying fit that her tears splashed down onto her mother's face.

She wiped them off her mother with mechanical motions of her hands.

"Child," said the father sympathetically and with obvious appreciation, "then what should we do?"

Gregor's sister only shrugged her shoulders, a sign of the hopelessness that, in contrast to her previous confidence, had come over her abruptly while she was crying.

"If only he understood us," said Gregor's father in a semi-questioning tone. Grete, in the midst of her sobbing, shook her hand energetically as a sign that there was no point thinking of that. "If he only understood us," his father repeated, shutting his eyes to absorb the girl's conviction upon the impossibility of this point, "then perhaps some compromise would be possible with him. But, as it is . . . "

"It must be gotten rid of," cried Gregor's sister. "That is the only way, Father. You must try to get rid of the idea that this is Gregor. The fact that we have believed this for so long, that is truly our real misfortune. But how can it be Gregor? If it were Gregor, he would have long ago realized that a communal life among human beings is not possible with such a stupid, dirty animal and would have gone away voluntarily, to be with his own kind. Then I would not have a brother, but we could go on living and honor his memory. But this animal plagues us. It drives away the lodgers, will obviously take over the entire apartment and leave us to spend the night in the alley. Just look, Father," she suddenly cried out, "he's already starting up again." With a fright that was totally incomprehensible to Gregor, his sister jumped back from their mother, pushed herself away from her chair, as if she would sooner sacrifice her mother than remain in Gregor's vicinity, and rushed behind her father who, alarmed by her behavior, also stood up and half raised his arms in front of Gregor's sister as though it were necessary to protect her.

But Gregor had no desire to create problems for anyone, certainly not for his sister. He had just started to turn himself around in order to crawl back into his room—quite a startling sight, since, as a result of his declining condition, he had to guide himself through the difficulty of turning around with his head, in this process trying to lift it but banging it against the floor several times. He could not help it—his neck spasmed and thrust him against the floor, and anyway his girth was getting much bigger now than the space in which he had to turn. He paused and looked around. His good intentions seemed to have been recognized; the fright had lasted only for a moment. Now they just looked at him in silence and sorrow. His mother lay in her chair, with her legs stretched out and pressed together, her eyes almost shut from weariness. His father and sister sat next to each other. Grete had set her hands around her father's neck.

"Now perhaps I can actually turn myself around," thought Gregor, and he began the task again. He couldn't stop puffing at the effort and had to rest now and then. Clouds of his fur wafted toward his mother, and she began to cough again.

No one was urging him on. It was all left to him on his own. When he had completed turning around, he immediately made toward his door. He was astonished at the great distance that separated him from his room and could not at all understand how, in his weakness, he had covered the same distance a short time before, almost without noticing it. Intent now on trotting along quickly, he hardly paid any attention to the fact that not a single word or cry from his family interrupted him.

Only when he was already in the door did he turn his head to look behind him—not completely, because his neck was quite limited in its range of motion by the accursed collar. At any rate, he saw that behind him nothing had changed. Only his sister was standing. His last glimpse brushed over his mother, who now appeared completely asleep. Hardly was Gregor inside his room, however, when the door was pushed shut quickly, bolted fast, and barred. He was startled by the sudden commotion behind him—so much so that his little limbs bent double under him. It was his sister who had been in such a hurry. She had stood up right away, waited, and then sprung forward nimbly; Gregor had not heard anything of

GREGOR HAD NO DESIRE TO CREATE PROBLEMS. HE REMEMBERED HIS
FAMILY WITH DEEP FEELINGS OF LOVE.

her approach. "Finally!" she cried out to her parents, as she turned the key in the lock.

"What now?" Gregor asked himself, looking around him in the darkness. He soon made the discovery that he could no longer move at all. He was not surprised at that. On the contrary, it struck him as unnatural that up to this point he had really been able to move around with these thin little legs supporting a body much bigger than even Josef K's had been. He did not want to guess at the meaning of it. Besides, he felt relatively content. True, he had pains throughout his entire body, but it seemed to him that they were gradually becoming weaker and weaker and would finally go away completely. He hardly even noticed the collar pulling tightly around his neck and the inflamed surrounding area, where his fur was entirely covered with white dust. His body grew around it, and in the mounds of fur the thing could hardly be seen. It pulled tighter; he could not feel it, not really. He remembered his family with deep feelings of love. He thought that he must disappear, and this decision was, if possible, even more certain than his sister's. He remained in this state of empty and peaceful reflection until the tower clock struck three o'clock in the morning. Through the window he witnessed the beginning of dawn outside. Then, without willing it, his head sank all the way down, and from his moist pink nostrils, over his still-beautiful fur, flowed out weakly his last breath. It seemed to him as the breath left him that he heard the great cat's song once more, and a circle of some kind seemed to shut within him.

EARLY IN THE MORNING the cleaning woman came. In her sheer energy and haste she banged all the doors—in precisely the way people had already asked her to avoid—so much so that, once she arrived, a quiet sleep was no longer possible anywhere in the entire apartment. In her customarily brief visit to Gregor, she at first found nothing special. She thought he lay so immobile there because he wanted to play the offended party; she gave him credit for as complete an understanding as possible. Since she happened to be holding the long broom in her hand, she tried to tickle Gregor with it from the door. When that was quite unsuccessful, she became irritated and poked Gregor a little, and only when she had shoved him hard without any resistance did she become concerned. When she quickly realized the true state of affairs, her eyes grew large, she whistled to herself. However, she didn't restrain herself for long. She pulled open the door of the bedroom and yelled in a loud voice into the darkness, "Come and look. It's kaput! It's just lying there, dead and done with!"

Mr. and Mrs. Samsa bolted awake in their marriage bed; they had to get over their startlement at the cleaning woman's abrupt shout before they managed to grasp what she was saying. But then they climbed quickly out of bed, one on either side. Mr. Samsa threw the bedspread over his shoulders, Mrs. Samsa came out only in her night-shirt, and like this they stepped into Gregor's room. Grete ran up behind them; she was fully clothed, as if she had not slept at all, which her white face also seemed to indicate. "Dead?" said Mrs. Samsa, and looked questioningly at the cleaning woman, as if she could not understand, although she could easily check for herself. "I should say so," said the cleaning woman and, by way of proof, poked Gregor's body with the broom once again, firmly. Mrs. Samsa made a movement as if she wished to restrain the broom, but didn't do it.

"Well," said Mr. Samsa, "now we can give thanks to God." He crossed himself, and the three women followed his example.

Grete, who did not take her eyes off the corpse, said, "Look how thin he was, really. He had eaten nothing for such a long time, yet he kept growing. The meals we put in here came out again exactly the same." In fact, Gregor's body looked surprisingly flat and dry—enormous, but bony and starved. That was apparent for the first time, now that he was no longer raised on his small limbs with his fur puffed outward and his whiskers no longer distracted one's gaze.

"Grete, come into our room for a moment," said Mrs.

Samsa with a melancholy smile, and Grete, not without looking back at the corpse, followed her parents into their bedroom.
The cleaning woman shut the door and opened the window
wide. In spite of the early morning, the fresh air was partly
tinged with warmth. It was already the end of March.

The three lodgers emerged from their room and looked
around for their breakfast, astonished that they had been forgotten. "Where's breakfast?" asked the middle one of the
gentlemen grumpily to the cleaning woman. She laid her finger to her lips and quickly and silently motioned to the
lodgers that they should come into Gregor's room. So they
came and stood in the room, which was already quite bright,
around Gregor's corpse, their hands in the pockets of their
somewhat worn jackets.

Then the door of the bedroom opened, and Mr. Samsa
appeared in his uniform, with his wife on one arm and his
daughter on the other. All were a little tear-stained. Grete
pressed her face onto her father's arm.

"Get out of my apartment immediately," Mr. Samsa said
to the lodgers; he pulled open the door to the hall, without letting go of the women. "What do you mean?" said the middle
lodger, sounding dismayed despite his sugary smile. The other
two men kept their hands behind them, constantly rubbing
them together as if excitedly anticipating a great squabble that

must end up in their favor. "I mean exactly what I say," replied Mr. Samsa, stepping directly with his wife and daughter up to the man. The lodger at first stood there motionless, then looked at the floor, as if matters were arranging themselves in a new way in his head. "All right, then, we'll go," he said, and looked up at Mr. Samsa as if, suddenly overcome by humility, he was asking fresh permission for this decision. Mr. Samsa simply nodded to him energetically, his eyes open wide.

The lodger immediately and decisively strode out into the hall. His two friends, who'd just been listening, hopped smartly after him, as if afraid that Mr. Samsa might step into the hall ahead of them and disrupt their bond with their leader. In the hall, all three of them took their hats from the coat rack, pulled their canes from the cane holder, bowed silently, and left the apartment. Mr. Samsa, in an unnecessary but determined show of suspicion, stepped with the two women out onto the landing, leaned against the railing, and looked over as the three lodgers slowly but steadily made their way down the staircase and disappeared around the turn. Once they vanished, the Samsa family lost interest in them, and when a butcher with a tray on his head arrived just then and, with a proud bearing, passed them on his way farther up the stairs, Mr. Samsa, together with the women, left the banister, and they all went, relieved, back into their apartment.

They decided to pass that day resting and going for a stroll. Not only had they earned this break from work, but there was no question that they really needed it. And so they sat down at the table and wrote three letters of apology: Mr. Samsa to his supervisor, Mrs. Samsa to her client, and Grete to her proprietor. While they wrote, the cleaning woman came in to say that she was leaving, for her morning work was finished. The family, busy writing, at first merely nodded, without glancing up. Only when the cleaning woman failed to depart did they look up angrily. "Well?" asked Mr. Samsa. The woman stood smiling in the doorway, as if she had a great stroke of luck to report to the family but would only do so if asked directly. The small, almost upright ostrich feather in her hat, which had irritated Mr. Samsa during her entire service, swayed lightly in all directions. "All right then, what do you really want?" asked Mrs. Samsa, whom the cleaning woman still usually respected. "Well," she answered, smiling so happily she couldn't go on speaking right away, "about that rubbish from the next room being thrown out, you mustn't worry about it. It's all taken care of." Mrs. Samsa and Grete bent down to their letters, as though they wanted to go on writing. Mr. Samsa, who noticed that the cleaning woman wanted to start describing everything in detail, put his hand out to silence her. Since she was not allowed to explain, she remembered the great hurry she was in, and called out, clearly insulted, "Bye-bye, everyone!" She turned around furiously and left the apartment with a fearful slamming of the door.

"This evening she'll be let go," said Mr. Samsa, but received no answer from either his wife or his daughter, because the cleaning woman seemed to have upset once again the tranquillity they had just attained. They got up, went to the window, and remained there, with their arms about each other. Mr. Samsa turned around in his chair in their direction and observed them quietly for a while. Then he called out, "All right, come here then. Let's finally do away with the old things. And have a little consideration for me." The women attended to him at once; they rushed to him, caressed him, and quickly ended their letters.

Then all three left the apartment together, something they had not done for months now, and took the electric tram into the open air outside the city. The car in which they were sitting by themselves was totally engulfed by the warm sun. Leaning back comfortably in their seats, they chatted about their future prospects, and they discovered that, upon careful observation, these were not at all bad, for all three of them had employment—which they had not really discussed with each other at all—that was extremely favorable and held promising prospects. The greatest improvement in their situation to come next, of course, had to be a change of dwelling. Now they planned to rent an apartment smaller and cheaper but better situated and generally more practical than the present one, which Gregor had found. As they occupied themselves with this talk, it struck Mr. and Mrs. Samsa, almost at the same moment, how their daughter, who was getting more animated all the time, had blossomed recently, in spite of all the troubles that had made her cheeks pale, into a beautiful and voluptuous young woman. Growing more silent and almost unconsciously understanding each other in their glances, they thought that the time was now at hand to seek out a good honest man for her. And it was something of a confirmation of their new dreams and good intentions when, at the end of their journey, their daughter got up first and stretched her young body.

## THE END

# Appendix

## The Curious Life of Franz Kafka, author of *The Meowmorphosis*

### By Coleridge Cook

Franz Kafka, arguably the most depressing writer ever to put pen to paper, was born into a middle-class Jewish family just outside Prague, in what was then Bohemia, the modern-day Czech Republic. By no means should this fact be taken to mean that he was a Bohemian in the modern sense of the word, though the term is technically correct.

His father, Hermann Kafka, was described, unsurprisingly, given his son's depiction of fathers in literature, as a "huge,

selfish, overbearing businessman"; Kafka called his father "a true
Kafka in strength, health, appetite, loudness of voice, eloquence,
self-satisfaction, worldly dominance, endurance, presence of
mind, [and] knowledge of human nature." One must then wonder how so much was lost in transmission to his slight, nervous
son and snigger in retrospect that the word *Kafkaesque* has come
to mean the profound absence of those virtues. Hermann was
the fourth child of Jacob Kafka, a ritual slaughterer of kosher
meats—showing that, from the beginning, the Kafkas were a
cheerful bunch—and came to Prague from Osek, a Jewish vil-
lage in southern Bohemia. In a great boon to biographically
minded literary critics everywhere, Hermann Kafka worked as
a traveling sales representative, establishing himself as an independent seller of men's and women's luxury goods and acces-
sories, employing several people and utilizing a large and
satisfied cat as his business logo.

Franz Kafka's mother, Julie, was the daughter of Jakob
Löwy, a prosperous brewer in Podebrady; she was better educated than her husband, though not than her son, who, as noted
above, would eventually have an adjective coined in his honor,
as much as his family members might be aggrieved to find that
their surname did not come to be a colloquial term for "pleasant" and "prosperous."

In summary: Little Franz was the scion of slaughterers,

fancy boutique salesmen, and brewers of alcohol, and of these he feared the fancy boutique owner as the manliest and most intimidating.

Franz was the eldest of six children. He had two younger brothers, Georg and Heinrich, who died at the ages of fifteen months and six months, respectively, before Franz was seven; and three younger sisters, Gabriele, Valerie, and Ottilie. On workdays, both parents were absent from the home, making little Franz a latchkey kid we can all identify with. (An animated musical film is rumored to be forthcoming, showing the young life of Kafka as a scamp with a cheeky word for everyone and a buoyant spirit no one can help but love. Gabriele, Valerie, and Ottilie have been cast as a trio of talking cats, for reasons that will soon become clear.) His mother helped manage her husband's business and worked long into the evening behind the counter; the children were left to their own devices under the casual eye of the occasional servant or governess.

Franz's relationship with his father was troubled, which certainly could not be surmised by anyone reading his works and counting up the good fathers on their fingers, then collapsing into a pit of despair when they find more unfeeling, evil father-devils than can be had in a Joss Whedon story.

Later, Kafka acquired some knowledge of French language and culture; one of his favorite authors was Gustave

Flaubert, who like Kafka never met a horrible circumstance that didn't thrill him to the bone. From 1889 to 1893, Franz attended the Deutsche Knabenschule, the boys' elementary school near the meat market. His Jewish education was lackadaisical, limited to his bar mitzvah at age thirteen and attendance at synagogue four times a year with his father; like any modernist child flirting with the sensual trends of nihilism, he did not enjoy this at all. After elementary school, he was admitted to the rigorous classics-oriented state gymnasium, Altstädter Deutsches Gymnasium, where he learned, wrote, and spoke German.

It was there that the cats first found him.

It began innocently enough: Stray cats, of which central Europe has no paucity, began to follow little Franz to school. At first he didn't notice, but eventually it became impossible to ignore as the stream of cats thickened and then began waiting outside his classrooms for him to emerge. The other students withdrew from Franz, recognizing perhaps the presence of a genius in their midst, or possibly a witch, or, even more possibly, someone who smelled altogether too much like fish. Kafka began to suspect all these things of himself as well, but since he had already decided that his father was a villain for the ages, he knew he could tell no one and would have to sort it out on his own.

Admitted to Charles-Ferdinand University in Prague, Kafka studied chemistry for a valiant two weeks before absconding for the law, since the literary opportunities offered by dark satires of the inner workings of chemistry are few. Law provided a range of career possibilities, which pleased his father and required a longer course of study, giving Kafka time to take classes in German studies and art history.

Like many university students, Kafka attended meetings of anarchist and anti-establishment clubs. Like many university students, his commitment to them was dependent on how many drinks he had had and whether he was on good terms with the treasurer that week. Hugo Bergmann, who attended the same elementary and high schools as Kafka, had a falling out with his feline-friendly classmate during their last academic year because "Kafka's bloody cats and my peace of mind just could not get along. The synthesis of cats and politics did not yet exist." Kafka sometimes wore a red carnation to school to show his support for socialism—or to look dapper, it is unclear which. He later stated, regarding the Bohemian anarchists: "They all sought thanklessly to realize human happiness. I understood them. But in the end human happiness was not really my concern, nor the aims of my writing, for books ought to be bludgeons to gouge out all our better parts rather than light entertainment. I was unable to continue marching alongside them for long without ... company."

He hoped that as he grew older his youthful feline magnetism would fade; yet the cats followed him and even increased their surveillance, taking up positions outside his dormitory and watching him through the night. Kafka began to show signs of mental deterioration, especially once the cats began to bring him presents in the form of pigeons and rats, conveniently exsanguinated for his use. He began to write tracts on the nature of the cat's soul; this brought him to the attention of the young thinker Max Brod, who unlike Kafka would go on to become a prolific, balanced, industrious, and well-liked writer of eighty-three works but, for mysterious reasons understood only by sociopathic cats and literary critics, would be remembered mostly for being his antisocial friend's literary executor.

Kafka obtained the degree of Doctor of Law on June 18, 1906, and performed an obligatory year of unpaid service as law clerk for the civil and criminal courts. Obviously, this internship had no effect on him whatsoever.

On November 1, 1907, Kafka was hired at a large Italian insurance company. He was unhappy with his working hours—the onerous and unusual shift from 8 a.m. until 6 p.m.—since it made it extremely difficult to concentrate on his writing. Indeed, the lack of sleep caused his personality to split; it was rumored that one side of Kafka's persona traveled around

Bohemia starting underground boxing clubs while the other side continued to work miserably as an insurance adjuster.

On July 15, 1908, he resigned and, two weeks later, found employment with the Worker's Accident Insurance Institute for the Kingdom of Bohemia, investigating the personal-injury claims of industrial workers and assessing compensation. From this we may assume that Kafka was surely well liked and had many genuine friends. According to several reports, Kafka invented the hard hat while working for this Bohemian OSHA—but an independent tribunal who claimed to have seen it all disputes the claim, since by then the poor man was obsessed with cats and their behavior and spent little time actually doing his job and quite a lot more cross-examining a certain Siamese.

Hounded from place to place by these cats who seemed to be driven by some weird mechanism to regard him as their personal deity, Kafka's work began to drift more and more toward the dark and paranoid instead of the light comedy sketches that had so delighted his university friends. Perhaps we lost a great comedian in that lost Kafka—a Bohemian Belushi, a Czech Carlin. Alas! But we must press on.

His father, angling for literary immortality as a wretched bastard, often referred to his son's job as insurance officer as a *Brotberuf* ("bread job," done only to pay the bills). While Kafka claimed loudly and to everyone who would listen that he despised the job, he was in fact a good worker, entrusted with compiling the company's annual report. As a sign of his skewed perception of the world and growing—shall we say, feline?—desire to torture others with the products of his mind, he was so proud of the results that he sent copies of this exciting business document to friends and family as holiday gifts. One may assume his father did not appreciate the gesture. The cats, however, who now numbered in the dozens and pressed into the legs of Kafka's trousers when he walked to work in the mornings, felt the report was well written and precise, though perhaps the sentences ran a little long.

Due to the split in his character discussed earlier, Kafka was reportedly able to remain committed to his literary work and boxing clubs. He and his friends were known collectively as the Little Prague Circle; they fought crime and wrote short modernist allegorical tales. Franz Kafka: insurance adjuster by day, literary rebel by night, and always, always the cats, watching him, watching him, and how could he focus on his comedy with their slitted, terrifying eyes on him and his father belching out pot roast and judgment at the dinner table? No, it would have to be something else, something more, a story, perhaps, about an animal who was not really an animal . . .

In 1911, his brother-in-law Karl Hermann fulfilled the

moral duty of brother-in-laws everywhere and asked Kafka to invest in a surefire scheme he had come up with, namely, the operation of an asbestos factory known as Prager Asbestwerke Hermann and Company. Kafka felt very good about this prospect at first, mainly because he knew nothing in particular about asbestos or how it reacts with minds already on shaky ground, and he dedicated much of his free time to the business. During that period, his writing became more and more, as Max Brod put it, "crazy pants."

Truly, Franz Kafka was a model for the modern office worker: deeply unhappy, but spending his weekends working on his "novel" and messing around with asbestos. Many employees of various corporations in our present world can take inspiration from the fact that this hero of the workers died alone and miserable, and, long after his death, a large number of equally unhappy people became obsessed with his work, to the point of literary critics being forced to find some merit in it, however they might have been more personally inclined to watch *Buffy the Vampire Slayer* and drink microbrews. I think it is safe to say he is an inspiration to us all.

IN 1912, MAX BROD introduced Kafka to Felice Bauer, who lived in Berlin and worked as a representative for a Dictaphone company. Over the next five years they corresponded a great deal, met occasionally, and twice were engaged to be married. Their relationship finally ended in 1917. That same year, Kafka began to suffer from tuberculosis—since the man could not catch a break with both hands, during his convalescence he was forced to live with his family, most notably his mother and sister Ottilie. We can assume that made no impression on his literary mind, and that Kafka was an unusually kind and large-hearted man, since his portraits of young women and sisters are so generous and subtle.

During this period, the cats suddenly vanished from his life—repelled by his illness or perhaps his literary output, Kafka could not be sure. He developed a terror of being perceived as repulsive both physically and mentally, though his mother assured him that he impressed everyone with his boyish, neat, and austere good looks, a quiet and cool demeanor, obvious intelligence, and dry sense of humor. Again, even the casual reader must be impressed with Kafka's visionary and forward-thinking approach to life, working a dead-end job, talking to a disinterested woman over long-distance communication, and living with his mother.

From 1920 onward Kafka developed an intense relationship with Bohemian writer Milena Jesenská. It did not last. In July 1923, during a vacation to Graal-Müritz on the Baltic, he met the improbably named Dora Diamant and moved to Berlin in the hope of distancing himself from his family's influence to concentrate on his writing. In Berlin, he lived in sin with Diamant, a 25-year-old kindergarten teacher from an orthodox Jewish family.

And the cats returned, this time a hardier breed of German forest cat, who insisted on watching though the windows whenever Kafka and Diamant made love, which really made everyone involved uncomfortable. Kafka began to observe and report on the behavior of the cats, keeping a notebook of their doings that would provide fuel for his more feline-oriented works. Indeed, it can safely be assumed that nothing Kafka ever wrote was actually about the behavior of humans—who, in general, behave like kindergarten teachers, journalists, and insurance adjusters rather than like sociopaths, which are mercifully rare. In cats, however, that psychic state can be considered standard factory issue.

Kafka's tuberculosis worsened in spite of his use of naturopathic treatments (which certainly shocks this biographer to the core), and he returned to Prague before receiving treatment in Dr. Hoffmann's sanatorium, near Vienna, where, given the state of European sanatoriums, it is perhaps better that he died on June 3, 1924, apparently from starvation. I think we can all surmise what occurred: The cats followed him to the hospital, and, knowing how much more grandly his work, which so beautifully showcased them, would be received after he died—a living modernist writer is essentially useless to anyone—they stole his food and devoured it themselves. His body was ultimately brought back to Prague, where he was buried on June 11, 1924, in the New Jewish Cemetery. If you were to visit today, you would find the place crawling with feral cats paying homage to their unhappy deity.

When Kafka died, he requested that his friend Max Brod destroy his unpublished works, writing: "Dearest Max, my last request: Everything I leave behind me [is] to be burned unread." However, Brod, a very good friend, ignored this request and instead published *The Trial*, *Amerika*, and *The Castle*. Upon signing the publication contracts, Brod let his hand fall onto the head of his own handsome cat, who looked well satisfied.

KAFKA'S WRITING attracted little attention until after his death, as is proper for any writer of worth. During his lifetime, he published only a few short stories and never finished any of his novels—as is proper for a prefigurer of the modern working male, unless of course *The Meowmorphosis* is to be considered a novel. If one looks carefully, however, one can see the cats of Prague creeping and crawling through all Kafka's stories, almost as though all these tales are one, and all concern one enormous, bewhiskered thing.

An interesting note regarding translation: Many translators point out that Kafka made great use of the peculiar German habit of moving verbs willy-nilly so that sentences sometimes spanned an entire page. Kafka's sentences thus deliver an unexpected twist just before the full stop—a twist that, like the discovery of Waldo in the upper corner of a carnival scene, illuminates the sentence as a whole. This is very irritating. The effect is achieved by the construction of the German language, which often requires the verb to be positioned at the end of the sentence. The translators insist these constructions cannot be duplicated in English—but that is mainly because they have been abused by schoolmasters and are now deathly afraid of the run-on sentence. A more truly insurmountable problem facing the translator is how to deal with the author's intentional use of ambiguous terms or words that have several different meanings. The cad! This biographer cannot believe that ambiguity and multiple meanings continue to be tolerated by modern readers.

One such instance is found in the first sentence of this very work, *The Meowmorphosis*. English translators have often rendered the word *Ungeziefer* as "insect" or "cockroach"; in Middle German, however, *Ungeziefer* literally means "unclean animal not suitable for sacrifice," or, as the clever and true thinker will recognize: *cat*.

# Discussion Questions

1. The name Samsa follows the same pattern of letters as Kafka. Do you think Kafka may have been trying to make a point here?

2. The manager notes that Gregor's work performance has lately been poor. Do you think his manager is just an ass? Or is it possible that Gregor is not quite the blameless victim in his own existence that he'd like to believe?

3. Is your manager an ass?

4. Gregor's sister Grete devotedly cares for him until she decides he doesn't appreciate it enough, at which point she grows sullen and decides she wants nothing more to do with him. Do you think she is mature enough to have a pet?

5. Gregor portrays his father as a lazy grumbler who needs to be rescued from financial misfortune by his intelligent, hardworking, professional son. Gregor also lives in abject terror of his father and will obey his every whim. What is wrong with this picture?

6. Gregor seems to have a great deal of trouble making decisions and sticking to them. It takes him half of Chapter 1 just to get out of bed; it's never clear whether he loves his sister deeply or is profoundly resentful of her; and, once he escapes the apartment, he delivers an entire soliloquy about appreciating his newfound freedom before ultimately turning around and going right back home again. Do you think Kafka is presenting insights into Gregor's character as a tormented individual or commenting on the basic psychology of cats as a species?

7. When Gregor meets the other cats of Prague, it doesn't take them long to sniff out the fact that he is a cowardly wretch who refuses to take responsibility for his own life. Do you think

humans are able to sniff out the same thing? How do you think you smell?

8. Gregor Samsa has some issues, doesn't he?

9. Franz Kafka had some issues, didn't he?

10. Dreams play a major role in this story from the very first line. Do you think Kafka intended us to read the entire story as a dream from which Gregor has not woken up? If so, do you think Christopher Nolan might be available to direct the movie?

# JOURNEY TO REGENCY ENGLAND—
# LAND OF THE UNDEAD!

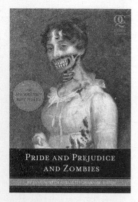

THE CLASSIC MASH-UP NOVEL
*Pride and Prejudice and Zombies*
By Jane Austen and Seth Grahame-Smith
ISBN 978-1-59474-334-4 • $12.95

A MOST PECULIAR PREQUEL
*Pride and Prejudice and Zombies:
Dawn of the Dreadfuls*
By Steve Hockensmith
ISBN 978-1-59474-454-9 • 12.95

A THOROUGHLY APPALLING SEQUEL
*Pride and Prejudice and Zombies:
Dreadfully Ever After*
By Steve Hockensmith
ISBN 978-1-59474-502-7 • $12.95